This Is The Life Vol. 2: Cold War

Published by Brewington & Carruth Publications

Copyright © 2020 by Tramena Carruth

This is a work of fiction. All characters, organizations, and events portrayed in this novel are either products of the author's imagination or are used factiously. Any similarity to persons living or dead is purely coincidental.

Identifiers: 978-0-578-64628-2(paperback)

10 9 8 7 6 5 4 3 2

This book is dedicated to Keyshawn La'Morris. I love you more than words. May you always dream big, and follow your heart. Love, Mommy

# *Acknowledgments*

First, I want to thank God. Without constant prayer and guidance I wouldn't have made it this far. Nothing that I ever do is without the love, that I receive and mercy that God has shown me throughout my life.

Keyshawn, my one and only baby boy. You mean the world to me, and I know that at 6 you really don't understand what it is that I'm doing, and why mommy is such an asshole, especially when she needs you to be quiet so that she can finish writing but one day you will. One day you will see that I'm literally doing everything that I can to make your life a little easier than mine. You have no idea that you were the saving grace for my life, and for that I owe you EVERYTHING!!!! Pinky promise double kiss.

My number one supporter, my personal promoting team, Mom. You have been so supportive throughout this process, and I truly do appreciate it. After years of writing and trying to figure out what I wanted to do, you've stuck by me through every process. Listening to the ideas that I have, and the stories that I want to write. I thank you for everything that you've done, and everything you will do. Keyshawn and I are forever grateful.

My brothers, Al, Vinny, and Makai. The annoyance is real!!! But I love you guys the most (not more than Keyshawn but you know). You three have been my heartbeats for as long as I can remember. They say siblings are the longest relationships you'll ever have, and I must say that the relationships I have with each one of you, while different, I wouldn't trade them for anything in this world.

My 88's Joy and Shay. Joy you've always been supportive, and you've been there through enough to know that the love I have for the "only white girl in the hood" is real. Shay, you've been more than a friend, and through this entire process we've grown close. You listen to me vent, you send me inspirational texts throughout the day (because you know that this Scorpio will stop writing completely). You won't let me give up on what we both know is my calling, my gift and I thank you for that.

***SHAMELESS PLUG TIME: If you're in the LA area and need a photographer, contact PhotoFrameLA.com. She's the best at what she does.

Coco, life and choices has put us in each other's lives. I may not be the perfect niece and at times I will surely shut down, and not talk to you, but you've always been there. Since '88, you've been right there. From taking me to see Darkness, to just riding around on stupid little missions that I wanted to go on, you've been there. When I wanted to cry over stupid men and everyday life,

you've been there to listen to me vent and never once judged. Thank you.

Darkness, you annoy my soul, but there's no one I would rather deal with than you. This thing of ours hasn't been easy, and it's not perfect but it's ours. If there's one thing I know, I'd rather spend the rest of the game of life and love with you, welcome to the end game.

My family and friends, thank you for supporting This is The Life Vol. 1, and being as supportive as you possibly could. From sharing posts on Facebook, and Instagram to buying the book itself. I am truly grateful, and fortunate to have people in my life who have decided to take this ride with me.

Letter to the readers:

I can't thank you enough for purchasing this book, and I can't express how grateful and fortunate I am that I've had people who would genuinely rock with me through this process.

The first time that I thought about writing was in high school, and I had written so many short stories and I didn't really know what I was doing, or if I wanted to make a career of this. Writing for me, like so many others, has been an outlet, a way for me to process the thoughts that seem to manifest in my mind.

When I started writing these stories about the Royals and the Senate, while based on the gangs in Los Angeles, I wanted to give them another perspective. I didn't want to name hoods, although I did in This is The Life Vol. 1, I just wanted them to be what they were initially supposed to be. I wanted them to be bigger than what they were. In this life we're all given a choice, and with that choice comes great responsibility.

I wanted the people of the Royals to be relatable, I wanted the characters to be relatable. I wanted you, the readers, to walk a mile in the lives of those who lived in those south-central streets, those who lived life by a code.

This is The Life Vol. 1, while it was my first baby, I know that I gave you guys a raw uncut version of what my writing was like, and with this one, I wanted you to be able to see that not only have I grown as a writer, but I've taken the time to actually put more of myself into this piece. I took everything that I had learned during that first process and applied it to my second novel and decided to give you all my everything.

I know that in this genre there are a lot of authors, and titles that you can read, and I'm forever grateful that you've decided to support me as I take you through my writing journey. I don't know what lies ahead but I do know that if you guys stick with me, I can only go further. I thank you for your love, support, and praise. Peace & Blessings.

I Love You All,

Tramena C.

# _Prologue_

London walked out of his office, closing the door behind her. Looking around the once filled office space, whose lights had been dimmed, and the only staff that remained was the janitor who was busy moving around the space wiping down the desks and emptying the garbage cans. The shades that covered the ceiling to floor windows had been drawn, leaving no visible peaks of the night sky that surrounded the city. Looking down at the gold Movado watch whose hands read seven thirty, she began making her way towards the elevator.

Her rich chocolate tone was clean, clear and free from blemishes or scars, standing five feet six inches but towering close to six feet tall due to the four-inch patent leather Christian Louboutin heels on her feet, almond shaped emerald green eyes that were covered by oversized Gucci frames. Dressed in a winter white knee length Alice & Olivia dress, with a black wrap trench coat by the same designer, three carat diamond studs donned her ears, and a ten-carat diamond solitaire with matching band on her ring finger.

Pressing her manicured finger on the call button summoning the elevator, the sounds of footsteps approaching behind her caused her to turn her head slightly in the direction. London watched as three men dressed in suits walked towards the office she had just left. Pulling her glasses down to the bridge of her nose and looking over the top. She saw him.

The tailored Tom Ford navy suit and freshly polished Gucci loafers were as familiar to her as the curves of her frame. Sliding the glasses back over her eyes, she turned away as they entered the office closing the door behind them.

Reaching into her purse removing her cellphone, she scrolled through the contacts landing on a number. Pressing the green phone button, as the elevator doors opened. London stepped inside, pressing her floor as the line trilled in her ear.

Rrrrrrrrinnnng. Rrrrrrrrinnnng. Rrrrrrrrinnnng.

"Long time no hear," the baritone boomed into her ear.

London was silent, as the sound of his voice began to stir the feeling's she had spent the better part of a year trying to ignore cascaded over her like a tidal wave in the middle of a storm.

"We have a problem," she said leaning against the metal railing inside of the mirror covered box.

He chuckled lightly, "Well damn. It's nice to hear from you."

Letting out an exasperated sigh London adjusted herself as the elevator stopped and chimed as the doors slid open.

"Black, I'm serious. Do you think that you'll be able to meet me?" she asked stepping off the elevator. Looking around the semi-empty parking garage, London reached into her purse removing her keys, and began heading towards her car.

"Whatever the fuck you into, count me out."

"I really need you to meet me, do you think that you can meet me at the old spot?"

"No," he answered flatly. "I haven't heard from you in what six months. You laid up over there with the enemy and now you want to meet. Where was all this meeting before you ran off with him? I'm good London, call that nigga."

London knew that calling Black was a risk, but she had too. Black had always been one to blow things out of proportion especially when it came to protecting the members of his family, the Royal's and he wasn't going to let anyone come in between the Family, even if she were still technically the Queen. The six months that she had spent avoiding Black would have to come to an end, especially if the feelings that were beginning to manifest in her gut were true. She needed him.

"Can we hash all of that out later," she asked. "I just really need to see you. You know that if I could talk freely over this phone I would. But, since I can't I need you to meet me."

"Unless you want me to help you bury that nigga you fucking, I'm not meeting you nowhere."

"Fuck it," she said standing in front of her car. "I'll come to you."

Black got silent and cleared his throat. "Meet me in the Nickerson's in two hours."

"Fine," she said as she silenced her car alarm.

"Don't have me waiting on you ma, for real."

"I won't," she said. "I'll be there."

"What the fuck did you do anyway?" he asked.

"I'll explain later," she said ending the call.

London opened the door to her black Range Rover, throwing her purse and phone on the passenger seat, before sliding into the car. Removing her heels as she closed the door, looking around the parking garage, and landing on the elevator banks. Thankful for the heavily tinted windows, and the six cars that surrounded her.

The space in which she was parked had a bird's eye view of the elevator banks. London wasn't moving from the space, and she wasn't leaving the parking garage until she saw his face and the faces of the men that he was with. Sliding her key into the ignition, turning off the car's headlights, and turning on the heated seat feature, she rested her head on the headrest and closed her eyes.

'I don't need this shit right now,' she thought.

"Call from… Karma," the automated voice came through the speakers. London looked at the digital screen and shook her head before answering the call.

"Hello," she answered. Sitting up in the seat and focusing her eyes on the elevators.

"What are you doing? Don't tell me you're still at that damn shrinks office," Karma's voice boomed through the speakers.

Reaching over and turning down the volume of the stereo. "No, I'm actually on my way to meet with Black."

"Wait, what?" she giggled.

London rolled her eyes knowing that she was going to have to tell Karma everything that had transpired that day, and although she needed to get it off her chest. She just didn't need to hear the criticism at least not at that moment.

London and Karma were first cousins and had been through their fair share of bullshit together. From house parties to designer bags, bamboo earrings, and fist fights. There wasn't a thing that they didn't know about each other and a thing that they didn't do together. While London was raised twenty-four miles from the south-central Los Angeles neighborhood that Karma lived, the two still spent every weekend together running the streets. Throughout the years and with all the drama that seemed to come their way it only made the bond they shared stronger.

Seven months separated the two in age with Karma being the oldest, and never letting London forget that age came before beauty. When London was voted Queen of the Royal's, an underworld organization that hailed from the streets of Los Angeles, she insisted on bringing Karma along with her on the ride she now calls hell.

"I'm going to need you to quiet down a little bit," she said in a hushed tone. "It's not what you think, trust me."

"Oh, please madame Cleo, tell me what it is you think that I'm thinking," Karma said in a sarcastic tone.

"I just watched Brandon walk into my psychologist office with two officers," London said letting out an exasperated sigh.

"Brandon? Officers?" she snapped.

"I don't know where they're from, and I didn't see a badge. But I do know for a fact that it was Brandon."

"Wait," Karma said. "Do you think it was LAPD?"

London shook her head. "If it were LAPD, I'm sure that I would've heard something by now. I think it's the feds."

"Damn London," she said. "Let me bring in Raven."

"No-" she started but was cut off when the line went silent. London's eyes darted towards the elevator, as she watched two women step off. The women were dressed in business attire and carrying leather satchels which gave her the inclination that they worked in the building. Laughing and engulfed in conversation she watched as they made their way down the ramp heading to their respective cars. London fumed as she continued to look towards the elevators, waiting for the men to descend.

"London?" Karma said coming back on the line. "Raven?"

"Yes," they both said in unison.

"What's going on?" Raven said. "I just left my office, and I'm tired as hell. I just want to make it home in time to finish setting up for the party tomorrow. So, Karma if this isn't pressing, I'm going to kill you."

Karma scuffed, "London's on her way to meet Black. Is that pressing enough for you?" The neck roll was evident in her tone.

"Don't tell me that the two of you have started back up again? We just got shit to at least look normal around the way," Raven said with a slight attitude.

"It's not like that Karma and you know it," London said removing the glasses that she was wearing. "It's not like that at all."

"Well can you fill me in because I think that I missed something," Raven said. The sounds of her keys jingling in the background could be heard followed by the chirping of her car alarm.

"Brandon's in my psych's office with two officers."

"London," Raven said in a soft tone. "Are you sure?"

"I think I would know what my husband looks like," London snapped. "Plus, he was wearing the suit I laid out for him this morning."

"What the fuck?" Raven snapped.

"Same thing I said," Karma chimed in. "London thinks that it may be the feds."

The line was silent for a while. Raven cleared her throat and continued, "Why would they be in your doctor's office? London what does your doctor know?"

"Not a lot," she answered. "But enough to get all of us locked under the jail."

"Fuck," Karma said.

"Doctor patient confidentiality," Raven replied. "That's what's going to protect you. Legally he can't divulge anything that you've said in his office. He's bound by laws and he can face a minimum of fifteen years in prison if he discloses anything that you've said in that office."

London shook her head. "They can and they will."

"As your attorney," Raven started. "I can look into this for you, but you know that it'll be a lot of red tape before I can figure out if your doctor has actually broken the law."

"I'll find out," she said.

"When are you supposed to meet with Black?" Karma asked.

"In less than two hours. He wants me to meet him in the Nickerson's," she answered.

"Do you want us to go with you?" Karma asked.

"I don't think that's a good idea. I kind of need to do this without y'all," London answered.

"Black is going to kill you if he thinks that you've ratted him or the family out. He already thinks you did when you ran off and married Brandon," Raven said.

London let out a frustrated sigh and frowned. There was no point in arguing with Raven, she was as strong willed as she was loyal. Raven and London had met while freshmen at Howard University, and had been thick as thieves ever since. Raven served as a member of the Royal Court, which happened to be London's counsel, as well as her attorney.

"Tell me you got something on that doctor," Karma said.

"No," London lied.

"I can't believe this shit," Karma said. "Just know that if that nigga is talking to the feds, I won't hesitate to kill him and everyone he knows."

The line beeping caused her to grab the phone off the seat. Looking down at the name that sprawled across the screen, *Hubby*, she frowned. "Hold on," she said sliding her finger across the screen answering the call.

"Hey honey," she said into the phone. "I was just thinking about you."

She rolled her eyes, as she rested her head back on the headrest. London wanted to question him as to what he was doing in her psychiatrist office but decided against it. She could always sense when something was wrong with him, and as she listened to the awkward silence, she could tell he was trying to feel her out.

"Where are you?" he asked breaking the silence.

"I had to make a stop before heading home."

"Do you think that you can pick up a bottle of wine? I forgot that Charlotte and Mark were coming over for dinner," he stated.

"Sure," she said. "I should be home within the hour."

"I love you."

"I love you," she said ending the call. London clicked over on the line and let out a sigh.

"What's the matter?" Raven asked.

London's eyes zoomed in with laser like precision as she focused on the three men stepping off the elevator. A devilish smirk crossed her face, as she watched them converse in front of the doors.

"I can't believe this shit," she said.

"What happened?" Karma asked.

"Brandon called," she said never taking her eyes off the men. "He asked me to pick up wine for dinner, which is odd being that we have a wine cellar."

"This nigga," Karma fumed.

"They're talking," London said. Turning the volume down lower than it was.

"Who?" Karma asked.

"Who do you think genius?" Raven snapped. "I wish we knew what they were saying."

"I can only imagine what they're talking about. It's no coincidence that this happens today," London said. "This has to be the dumbest thing that I've ever done."

"What exactly did you do?" Raven asked.

"Started seeing a shrink for one," she said. London watched as the three men shook hands and parted ways. Brandon's red Mercedes came around the corner and headed for the exit, followed by a black Crown Victoria with police issued tinted windows.

"Damn," she whispered shaking her head. Reaching over on the dashboard pressing a button causing the dash to slide open.

"There's no shame or blame in you trying to get help. You've had one hell of a year," Raven said.

"Hell, it's been a fucked-up couple of years," Karma added.

"They're gone," she said removing the contents of the compartment. Checking to make sure that everything was secure, knowing that everything that happened from this moment forward would alter the way in which she lived her life.

"Ok," Karma said. "That's good, right?"

"London, you're out. As of this day and every day after this you're out, at least until we can figure out how to handle this," Raven said.

"You're never out," she said.

"What?" Karma said.

"My dad told me that right before he died. He said that no matter what. You're never out. You can wipe the board clean and start a new game, but at the end of the day. It's always the same game, and even if the players do change. The old ones are still playing, so you're never really out."

Karma sighed, "We're going to be there when you meet Black."

"Why?" London asked.

"Because you're becoming unhinged," Karma said with an attitude. "And you know that if Black senses something is wrong, he will not hesitate to take matters into his own hands, and that's something that we don't need."

She scuffed, "Fine. Meet me in an hour in the Nickerson's."

"Why an hour? It should take you less than twenty minutes since you're already downtown," Karma questioned.

"I gotta go take care of some shit with Dr. Nichols," she answered. "Just meet me there."

"Aight," Karma said.

"London," Raven started.

"Yeah."

"In this to the end," she said.

"In this to the end."

"Aight bitches. One hour," Karma said.

Ending the call and placing her shoes back on her feet she stepped from the car and made her way towards the elevator. She made a mental note of the cars in the lot, as she pressed the button and waited for the doors to open.

———————————————————————

Standing in the opened doorway Dr. Richard Nichols watched as the three men filed into the elevator, and grimaced. Shaking his head wondering how he had sunk so low in his life. Coming to an inconclusive conclusion he closed the door once the elevator doors closed. Leaning against the wall of his office, taking in a deep breath. The stench of perfume, cologne, and cigarette smoke lingered in the air.

He had been a practicing psychologist for over ten years and had built a lucrative business for himself, catering to many but as of late his client list were filled with housewives. Many of the women who had visited his office all longed for adult connection. His latest patient and one of the reasons for the incessant visits from the men in suits had been one of the most beautiful, diabolical women he had ever met.

For six weeks he'd watch as she would come into his office, weeks where she would sit in the chair opposite his desk, and never say more than a word. Although he wanted to know why the woman who had spent thousands of dollars never seemed to take advantage of his services, and after today he understood completely. He had been given the gift into the scandalous life that she lived, ultimately leading to a decision that he didn't want to make. A decision that ethically, and professionally would destroy him and his career.

'What the hell did I get myself into?' he thought as he turned off the lights and walked towards his desk. Taking a seat in the oversized swivel office chair, he reached into the bottom drawer of his desk removing a bottle of Scotch.

'If only I had taken that deal months ago,' his subconscious screamed. Removing the top from the bottle before turning it towards his lips. Taking a swallow from the half empty bottle, his eyes landing on the picture frames that sat casually atop his teak wood desk.

His office hadn't been decorated with expensive art, and mountains of psychology books. What he lacked in modern décor; the view that overlooked the downtown Los Angeles skyline made up for it. As he glared at the frames holding the images of his wife, Margarette, and his daughter, Claire, thoughts of how he was going to explain the current dilemma to them.

The squeaking the door made when it opened caught his attention, her perfume assaulted his nostrils and flowed through the air as casually as it had from the first day that he had met her. Her silhouette dancing from the moonlight displaying her hourglass curves and painting them on the wall. The sounds of her heels tapping lightly across the floor, causing him to look up from the picture frames, and look at the woman standing in the room.

"I didn't need any of this in my life," he said looking at her. Taking a drink from the bottle before slamming it on the desk.

"Ssssshhhh," she said placing a finger to her full lips. "Who were they? And what do they know?"

"I didn't tell them anything," he said. His eyes began shifting around the room, trying to land on any object other than her. London watched as he began tapping his hand on the desk in a rapid pace, a sign that he was nervous.

"That's funny," she said. "I never said that you told them anything. What do they know Richard?"

London looked at him and frowned. On another day she would've sworn that he was the doppelganger for Matthew McConaughey, with his sandy brown hair, chiseled features, and boyish good looks, but today with the color draining from his face, and the dishevelment of his appearance she wouldn't have given him a second glance.

He looked at the woman and for the first time since she walked through the door, he felt as though prison was the furthest thing from his future. London had traded in her oversized glasses and handbag. Wrapped in her perfectly manicured hand was a Ruger .380 handgun.

"What do they know?" she asked raising the gun. "Why were they here?"

"Lo… Lo… London," he stammered. "I didn't tell them anything. I don't know what you're thinking but it's not what you think."

"Richard," she said pointing the gun at his head. "The District Attorney doesn't make house calls unless there's a case, and he needs to be certain that there's enough evidence to pursue the matter. I find it rather convenient that today, of all days he shows up, flanked by two officers who I assume aren't from around here. What agency?"

His eyes began shifting around the room, as he took another sip from the bottle. After hearing only a snippet of what she was capable of he knew that he was no match for her. The woman was beautiful, smart, and dangerous. A sociopath was his initial diagnosis, and from the looks of things he was correct in his prognosis.

"The… they…they're from the DEA," he replied.

His cheeks turned beet red as the sting from the liquor made its way down his throat, giving him the false illusions that he needed now to withstand the impending doom that surrounded him.

"What do they want with you?" she asked.

"They want you and the people that work for you. If everything that you've said and everything that they know happens to be true."

"What else? How long have they been coming here?" she asked taking a seat in the chair across from him. Never lowering the gun. "I've been in this business for a long time, and for years the feds have been around. But never have I had to worry about feds this close. To see them coming and going from your office on the same day that I decide to talk to you. It makes me wonder. What do they have on you? And what did you tell them about me?"

Richard thought about lying, but the look that was in her eyes said that he shouldn't. Her green eyes were trained on him in a way that he hadn't seen before, and the gun that was in her hand didn't waiver from the position she had pointed it in, which was his head.

"They saw you during your first visit," he said. "Initially they were investigating me for opioid prescriptions that I had written, but when they saw you, I was offered a deal."

"What was the deal? Me for you?" she asked.

"London, I don't know you," he said as he polished off the rest of the bottle. "But I can tell you that they're building a case against you. They offered me full immunity if I could get them the information, they needed to take you and your organization down."

"So, it's either me or you?"

"Lon...Lon...London you have to understand-"

London raised her free hand signaling him to stop speaking. "I need you to understand something. This," she said waving the gun between them. "This is my life and I've built everything around me. From the people in my Family, even the people that think for some reason they have free will. Los Angeles belongs to me, from the skyscrapers to the politicians, down to the local businessman, even the psychologist who's clearly gotten way over his head."

"What does that mean?" he asked in a shaky tone.

"Loyalty is everything when it comes to family. If a family doesn't have loyalty then they're all better off dead," she said repeating the phrase she had heard several times throughout her dealings. Standing from the seat she lowered the gun and walked over towards the window and looked over the skyline. The lights flickering around the city caused a smile to come to her face.

"Richard Nichols," she said turning towards him. "Or should I call you Michael Villa, youngest son of Salvador Villa. Head of the Villa Organization. Your address is 1214 E Tujunga Ave, Burbank."

"How… how…how do you know any of that?" he asked looking from her to the frames that sat on his desk.

"Thirty years ago, you were relocated and placed into witness protection," she said turning away. "Did you really think that would separate you from the life you were born into?"

'She's the devil,' he thought. 'She has to be. There's no way that she should know anything about me. I've covered all of my steps, carefully.'

"Your father's a dear friend of mine," she said seemingly reading his thoughts.

Richard no longer wanted to be in the room with her, the space in which the two were didn't seem like enough room for them both. He didn't know where she had come from, and he didn't care. At that moment he wanted his life to go back to what it was six weeks ago. Six weeks before the beautiful serpent stepped into his office. But there was no reset button when it came to life. As he sat in his chair remembering the world that he had once known it finally donned on him, all criminals knew one another.

"Non puoi uccidermi.," he said in Italian. 'You can't kill me.'

"I can, and I will," she said just above a whisper. "But not yet. You know the beginning. Now let me take you through the rest. Because, tonight just might be the last night either of us live."

# *2015*

# *Chapter One*

Sitting on the passenger side of her Jaguar as Black pushed the car to its limit, weaving in and out of what was left of the nightly traffic, London's mind reflected on the day's events.

The day had already been a stressful one, within a twelve-hour span London had discovered that many of the original members that sat on the Board of the Royals were the very ones who ran the Senate, their rivals. Ultimately ending with London ordering the deaths of every member that sat in the conference room of the funeral home that the impromptu meeting was held and leading to a chain of events that would forever alter the way people saw her, including Black.

The meeting that they had just left with her ex-boyfriend had been a disaster. What should've been a casual sit down, turned into her demanding that Don leave LA and never return. When he asked for half a million dollars, she knew that having him leave the city wouldn't suffice. London needed him to disappear, and not just disappear from her life but from all existence.

After telling Black that she wanted Don killed, she learned that there was a plan in motion to have the man who once was the love of her life executed. London saw it as a means to an end while her counterpart, Black, saw it as a way to eliminate all competition when it came to the matters of London's heart.

Staring aimlessly out of the window, watching the cars they passed, exit signs, and cement filled dividers as the silence that enfolded the car was enough to scream the thoughts that filled both of their heads.

Before walking into the bar Raven had told them of her suspicions of Sade. Sade was one of London's best friends, and although she hadn't been given the opportunity of joining the Royal's like Karma and Raven, London still considered her a close ally.

From the moment she had met Sade they were close, London being an only child seemed to click with the girls she had met in college forging a friendship that they hoped would withstand the hands of time. But, when Raven dropped the bomb that Sade could possibly be an informant, her vision of the woman she considered a sister became less clear.

Sade was smart, beautiful, and a successful real estate agent. While in college she like the rest of the world had learned that her parents were behind several Ponzi schemes, that racked in millions of dollars a year, and led to them being indicted by the Federal Government who sentenced them both to fifteen to twenty years in prison. After what happened to her parents, Sade had vowed not to follow in their footsteps. Creating a family with her friends she wrote her parents off and hadn't looked back. While London knew that Sade had it rough the past couple of years, she also knew that there was no bond greater than a child and their parents. Giving Raven's statement about Sade wearing a wire legs to grow.

While she had never discussed the family in front of Sade, that didn't stop her from asking questions about

London's assets as well as her parents. Sade had always been an inquisitive person, and London had always played her hand close to her chest when it came to anyone, but as of late everyone who wasn't involved in the Royal's wasn't privy to London's personal life, Sade included.

The trusting spirit that London once had, had been replaced by skepticism for those in her life, Sade was no exception. While it didn't surprise her when Raven shared her suspicions about Sade, because she had suspected as much. The vibes that she had received from Sade didn't mesh well with her spirit as of late and caused her to keep her distance. Other than phone calls, and the occasional outing London and Sade hadn't so much as been in the same room with one another alone She made sure that either Karma or Raven would be accompanying them. Earlier in the day, while Sade was showing London houses in the Manhattan Beach suburb, London had to end the tour early due to the vibes that she received from Sade's aura.

Even if she couldn't be sure that Sade was in fact an informant and had intended on turning states witness against them, Raven had made the mistake of dropping that bomb in front of Black and Vine. Whether there was proof or not she knew that Sade's days were indeed numbered.

Pulling into the driveway of his house, Black turned off the ignition and leaned back in the seat. Turning in his seat so that he faced London. The white sheer blouse that she wore displayed the black push-up bra underneath, and the black leather pants she wore looked as though they were painted on hugging her curves.

The moonlight that entered the car reflecting off her chocolate skin kissing her gently giving her the look of the goddesses from those African American paintings that were sold on the street corners.

He wanted her. Not just sexually, like many of the women he had been with in his life. No, he wanted London whole heartedly. He wanted to wake up to her in the morning and go to sleep with her at night, dinners by candlelight, and trips to different countries on whims. From the moment that he saw her at the airport he wanted her, and when fate dealt the cards putting them in one another's space he knew that it was only a matter of time before they would be together.

But, as luck would have it, it never happened. The three months that Black had known London the two hadn't spent much time alone. While they were voted King and Queen of the family, it did nothing to bring them together. Other than the kiss that the two had shared, nothing seemed to happen between the two. Leaving him to continue to fuck with the women around the way, who only seemed to fill his bed but never his heart.

"What's on your mind?" he asked placing his arm around the back of her seat.

She sighed and turned her body towards him. "You ever get the feeling that this is more than it's worth," she asked looking at him. "Everything around us just might come crashing down. It's like one thing after another."

"It's nothing that we can't handle," he said. "We can only take care of one thing at a time."

"Easier said than done," she said. Adjusting herself in the seat, removing the seat belt that held her captive.

Black watched as she leaned against the door, pulling one of her legs into the seat. "Finding out the Board was flawed was one thing, and now this with Sade. This is a whole other pill that I don't know if I can swallow."

"Is it though?" he asked locking eyes with her.

Black hadn't known much about Sade, only that she was one fourth of the crew, and the only female that London hadn't brought in to become a part of her Royal Court. When he had saw her in passing it always puzzled him, how she wasn't a part of the family. After what Raven had said he now wondered what the next move would be when it came to her friend.

"It would be," she said diverting her eyes.

"I always found it odd that you never brought her around, I never questioned it because it wasn't my place. Whatever happens between you and your girls, is just that between you and your girls."

She shrugged, "Is she really my girl? If what Raven suspects turns out to be true."

"Closed casket," Black said. His tone was sharp, clear, and dripping with disdain. London had watched Black over the months and knew that he would have rather died a thousand deaths than to have anyone come for the Royal's.

It didn't matter that Sade and London were friends, many of the people who he considered friends had all but turned out to be foes, so there was no room in his heart for disloyalty.

London looked at him perplexed. "Sade has always been nosy, and I know that what Raven said is starting to cause all kinds of red flags and tempers to flare. But let's be real, Sade knows nothing about the family. I don't think a 'closed casket' is necessary at this time."

"The trust between y'all has already been altered, regardless if you want to admit it or not. But that shit is gone and there's no coming back from that," he said.

"Not completely," she countered.

Black sighed and leaned back. "What happens when you find out that your girl is an informant? You gon' handle the situation or are you going to sweep it under the rug."

"Just give me time to figure out what's what," she said noticing the headlights from behind them. "Everybody shows their hand in due time, right?"

Black shook his head in agreement and opened the car door. Leaning down in the car he locked eyes with her. "Just know that if I find out that your girl is wired up, there's nothing that you can do to stop me from canceling her ass."

"I know," she said as he closed the door.

London stepped out of the car and watched as the others parked in front of the house and filed out of theirs. Walking behind Black towards the house, waiting for him to open the door and stepping in.

The smell of weed mixed with a glade plug-in filled the air. She removed her heels and headed for the couch. Taking a seat, she sprawled out on the Italian leather couch placing her arm over her eyes.

"Ok," Karma said walking through the door. "This shit is getting crazier by the second, we need to find the mothafucka that's behind LA Confidential because this is the type of negative energy I don't need."

"What now?" London groaned as she sat up. Karma walked over towards her, throwing her cellphone onto the space next to her hitting her leg as it landed.

*Tis the season to be jolly. Let's just say that this holiday season has been nothing but giving. We've received reports that there's a new Board of the Royal's all thanks to the Queen, who single handedly removed all the old players. There's no word as to why this decision has been made, but we're sure that time will tell. It seems as though our Queen has learned from the best of the best. We wonder what her father would say once he realizes*

*that the daughter that he raised is now worthy of the*
*namesake bestowed upon her. Soon you'll hate me*
*LA Confidential.*

"I'm too tired to even give a damn," she said handing the phone back to Karma. "I'll worry tomorrow about who's behind the site. Tonight, let's just have a drink smoke a few blunts and go to sleep."

"Fuck that," Karma said taking a seat next to London. "What's up with the people you talked to? You think they'll be able to track down the person."

London shrugged. "I only talked to them, and I couldn't even go into specifics. So, no I don't think they'll be able to track down the person behind the site. At least not yet."

"What's going on?" Raven said walking over towards them. Taking a seat on the sofa opposite them she nodded towards Black, and Vine before removing a pack of blunts from her purse and a container that held her weed.

"The emails that have been coming out for the past couple of days," Karma said looking at her. "We need to find out who's behind the site, and have it removed before shit gets really bad."

"I know some guys from school that can probably find out who's behind the site. It won't be cheap," she said looking around the room. "But they can get the shit done."

"Cool," Karma replied. "Talk to them and get this shit over with because I for one am tired of my phone buzzing for all the wrong reasons."

"This can't be life," London said leaning her head back.

"This is life," Vine said taking a seat on the arm of the couch. He looked at every girl in the room, and then Black. "It's fucked up and none of us thought that this would be the outcome of joining the Royals but it's our reality."

"What's this shit about Sade, Rave? You know you can't just throw out accusations with no follow up," London said looking at her.

Raven rolled the blunt and used her lips to seal it. Taking a lighter that was on the glass-top coffee table lighting it, taking in a deep pull she exhaled the smoke.

"I wouldn't put a thing past anyone these days," Raven said. "As far as I'm concerned, Sade is just a liability at this point. She serves no purpose to any of us. To be honest none of us has really even rocked with her since we joined this shit. So we really don't know what's going on with her."

"Damn," Karma responded. "We've really been feeding her with a long-handled spoon, and none of us have a real reason to think Sade would turn state on us. She knows nothing."

"Clearly she knows nothing about the Royal's, but she knows something," Raven said expelling smoke.

"Otherwise she wouldn't be so concerned with London and her parents."

"What you mean?" Vine asked.

Raven passed him the blunt and pushed an unruly strand of hair from her face. The white pants suit that she wore tailored to her body, and the pink button up shirt had been unhooked by three buttons displaying the mounds of her white breasts, and two gold chains that draped around her neck.

"Sade's parents are in the feds looking at football numbers," she said leaning back on the couch. "I wouldn't be surprised if she was doing something for them, or at least something she thought would help them and their situation."

Karma looked at Raven and frowned, her perfectly arched eyebrows connecting. "It's all speculation," she said looking from Raven, Vine, Black and landing on London.

"Yeah it is," Raven countered. "But a lot of cases have been made and won based on speculation."

"We should at least see if there's something behind this," London said looking at her. "Black and I already spoke about the situation and before shit goes left, I want to know the real."

Karma raised her index finger silencing them and turned towards Black. "If this shit goes left, which it very well may. Closed casket?"

"It's the only way I know," he said looking at everyone in the room. Black turned and walked through the dining area before disappearing into the kitchen. The room grew eerily quiet as the only sounds to be heard were of the cabinets opening and glasses being moved around. Karma cleared her throat and looked at her girls.

"Alright case closed," Karma said. "Now back to you. You think you passed this time, because at the point we're going one of us is going to be needing a lawyer."

Grabbing one of the throw pillows next to her Raven threw it towards Karma and giggled. "I hope so," Raven said flipping her off.

"Good," Karma said. "Third times a charm. Now London what's this shit with the Board. Is what the site saying about the Board members being killed true."

"Ugggghhhhh," she groaned and frowned. "You know how we've been going toe to toe with the Senate for control over several of our areas."

"Yeah," Karma replied.

"Turns out the Board knew all about it, because they were the damn Senate."

Karma and Raven looked at one another and then towards London. It never occurred to them that the Senate had been ran by the Original's, hell it never occurred to any one for that matter. Now that the revelation had been made, it all started to make sense.

"So, what's the move?" Raven asked.

"We rebuild," London said in a flat tone. "I don't know who to trust and I really don't feel like bringing in anyone that had dealings with the old members, so from this point forward the Board consist of us. Me, Black, Vine, you two, and Face. I don't have time to vet new members and I don't have time to try to worry about who's going to cross me next."

"In this to the end," Karma said taking the blunt from Vine.

"In this to the end," Raven and London said in unison.

Vine stood from his seat and walked towards the kitchen leaving the girls alone to continue talking and smoking in the living room. Walking into the kitchen he headed towards the refrigerator opening the door and removing two bottles of beer. Sliding one across the counter towards black, who was sitting at the island on a bar stool.

"What are you thinking about my nigga?" Vine asked as he opened the bottle taking a swig from the beer. Rolling up the sleeves of the long-sleeve black shirt that he was wearing, before reaching into his pocket pulling out a blunt and canister.

He looked over at his boy and smirked. It didn't take a genius to realize that the wheels were spinning in Black's mind. He had stood to the side and listened as the women talked freely as if he weren't in the room, as if they weren't in his house. Black had a way of becoming quiet and withdrawn when he was deep in thought, and as

Vine stood there looking at him, he knew that there was something brewing behind the dark eyes of his partner in crime.

Black opened the beer throwing the top on the counter and taking a sip. "How soon can we put somebody on Sade?"

"Tonight, if you want," Vine smiled knowing where the conversation was headed.

"Get somebody on that bitch, and not a word to London or Karma. I know how yo ass like to pillow talk," he said smirking.

"Fuck you cuz," he said with a chuckle. "What about your girl? What you gon' tell her?"

"I'll bring her in once I find out what I need to know."

Vine shook his head in agreement as he used his pinky nail to open the blunt. Removing the tobacco into the garbage can he placed it on the counter, opening the canister placing three buds into the blunt before breaking them down.

"You know baby just aint gon' sit by idly while you do all the work," Vine said looking at him.

"At this point she's gon' have to play her role."

"You remember the first time you smelled blood, my nigga. That same look that every nigga that has caught a body had written across their faces the very first time, look at London and tell me she doesn't have that look."

Black looked at him and frowned, "Nigga we all know that what went down can be a fluke."

Vine chuckled lightly, "Not when it comes to her. Any other bitch I'd agree but when it comes to her. That bitch is the real deal nigga. Don't let that sheltered shit fool you, the bitch was raised by Stone, there aint no telling what she's capable of."

Vine watched as Black downed the rest of his beer and lit the blunt. Taking a deep pull exhaling the smoke and passing it to his boy he continued. "On the drive over did she order the hit on that nigga from the bar."

Black shook his head yes. "But you know that shit was already in the works before we pulled off the block."

"You know that, and I know that, but did she order the hit before or after you told her that it was a done deal," Vine pressed.

"Before," Black answered.

"Then my young nigga you're looking at the making of the female version of you. That broad aint gon' let shit come in between her and the family. All she needed was the push to surface, and now that she has, shit's looking really different."

"What are you saying?"

Vine took the blunt back from him and took a pull from the blunt before continuing, "This shit was a match made in hell. Welcome home cuz."

London walked into the kitchen and looked from Vine to Black. They were deep into a conversation about plans for New Year's, passing a blunt between them. The empty beer bottles that littered the counter space gave her the impression that they were blitzed and well on their way to being done.

Walking over to the cabinet, removing a glass and placing it on the counter she could feel the eyes burning a hole into her. Turning around to see Black staring at her she smiled and folded her arms across her chest.

"So," she said looking at him. "What are y'all talking about?"

"Yo psychopath ass," Vine laughed.

London turned around and opened the refrigerator grabbing the gallon of water and pouring a glass. "I'm the psychopath. This coming from the nigga that tortured Jamal over five hundred dollars," she said with an attitude.

"That was business," Vine capped. "And it wasn't torture. It was just a reminder, that you can't miscount niggas money and expect to still have two good hands."

"Is that what we're calling it," she said placing her hand on her hips. She grabbed the cup off the counter and took a sip from the cup.

"What's wrong?" she asked looking at Black. His eyes were glossed over thanks to the weed and beer he had been drinking, and the look on his face was as if he were seeing her for the first time.

"Let me talk to you upstairs," he said. She watched as he stood from the barstool and headed out of the kitchen. London watched as he disappeared and turned towards Vine.

"What does he want with me?" she whispered looking at Vine.

Vine shrugged and placed the end of the blunt he was smoking into the empty beer bottle. Standing to his feet, rubbing his hand over his jeans he looked at her and smiled.

"Probably some pussy," he said in a casual tone. "I know I'm about to go get me some."

Vine walked out of the kitchen leaving London alone. The words echoed in her head, as she finished the cup of water she had been cradling in her hand. As bad as she wanted to have sex with Black, London didn't know if she was ready to go there with him, at least not yet.

It had been a while since she had been intimate with a man, and with the way her last relationship ended she didn't know if sex was the right move for her at this point in her life. Over the past few months since the two had known each other Black had never pressed her for sex. He'd always been respectful, honest, and an all-around gentleman.

London couldn't help that she was overthinking things, which she often did when it came to Black. Not knowing whether being intimate with Black would lead to the path of destruction that in the past almost always stemmed from one night of sex.

Placing the glass in the sink she walked out of the kitchen and into the living room. Noticing that Karma had ducked off with Vine, leaving a sleeping Raven on the couch. London walked towards the couch, grabbing the throw that was on the back of the love seat covering her. Looking towards the door, making sure that the door was locked she began ascending the stairs.

"Black," she called out. She looked around the dark hallway unsure as to what room he was in. On her initial visit London hadn't been given a tour of the upper level, and as she looked around the dark hallway with her hand on the wall in a desperate attempt to find the light switch. The door at the end of the hall cracked just enough to provide minimal light into the hallway. As she walked down the hall, the sounds of Karma's giggles and Vine's baritone came through one of the closed doors, causing her to shake her head.

"Anytime, anyplace,' she thought. Letting out a sigh as she pushed open the door at the end of the hall. Nerves seemed to manifest within her causing her to regret climbing the stairs in the first place. The overhead lights were out, and the only light that shown in the room came from the opened bathroom door.

Wall to wall plush black carpet filled the room, a four poster California king-size bed with a glass paneled nightstand on either side. An oversized navy colored comforter covered the bed, eight pillows stacked against the headboard, sheer drapes covering the double doors that led to the patio area, the opened walk in closet displaying racks of clothes and clear plexiglass shoe containers that were stacked against one side of the closets wall.

London stepped into the room, closing and locking the door behind her. She walked over towards the bed and climbed atop. She sprawled atop the comforter, inhaling the smell of Black's cologne that was embedded within the fabric.

London peered over her shoulder looking towards the bathroom. The sounds of the water running into the tub had caught her attention, and as she watched him leaning over the tub feeling the water, she couldn't help but smile.

'It's going to happen,' her subconscious screamed.

"Come here," he said standing in the doorway. Wiping his hands with the white hand towel as he looked at her.

London stood from the bed and walked over towards him. Throwing the towel to the floor, he reached over and began unbuttoning her shirt.

"What're you doing?" she asked in a shaky tone. As his hands gently touched her skin causing her to shiver goosebumps rode up her bare skin, as the shirt dropped to the floor.

"About to give you a bath," he said as the shirt fell to the floor. He reached around unhooking her bra. Black smiled displaying all thirty-two of his pearly whites, as he watched her place her arms across her chest, covering her firm 36-D cup breasts.

"Black I don't think-" she started but was silenced by a kiss. Wrapping her arms around him as she kissed him deeply, allowing him to freely roam his hands over her back and down her behind.

"I don't wanna do shit to you that you don't want me to," he said in between kisses. "Let me know when you want me to stop."

Black's hands slid around the front of her pants as he unbuttoned and removed the leather pants that she was wearing. Sliding his hands over her lower body noticing that she wasn't wearing any panties, casually sliding over the front of her body landing on her neatly shaved pussy.

Taking a step back he watched as the once confident woman he had known throughout the months, who was now bare and completely nude, tried desperately to cover her lady parts with her arms and hands.

"Black," she said looking at him.

Black chuckled noticing the awkward stance that she was in. She was perfect, to him. From her firm breast, small waist, and round ass. Even the stretch marks that had covered her ass cheeks and hips were perfect, and watching her covering herself, he knew that for as beautiful a woman as she was, she was still as insecure as the next.

Walking over towards the tub, turning off the water. He grabbed her hand, helping her climb into the bubble filled jacuzzi tub. Pressing a button on the side powering the jets, he watched as she slid into the hot water, leaning her head back onto the neck pillow and relaxed.

London watched as he removed his clothes. His black skin was as dark as the night sky and lay perfectly on his six feet four muscular build, tattoos covered his chest, arms, and back, and as he removed the Calvin Klein boxers that he was wearing London looked down at the thick member that swung between his legs. He stepped into the water with her, pushing her legs open so that he could sit between them, leaning his head back against her chest and closed his eyes.

He had lived in the house for over two years and had never had a reason to take a bath, and he had never allowed a woman into his home never really giving himself the opportunity. London placed her hand on his chin causing his face to turn towards hers, she leaned forward and kissed his lips. Feeling his hand inching up her thighs, finding their way to her love box.

"It's been a while," she said between kisses.

Black stopped kissing her and looked into her eyes. "I got you. Tell me when you want me to stop."

Black scooted forward in the tub and in one swoop pulled London on top of him. London landed on top of him with her anatomy lining up with his perfectly.

"Wait," she said as she rested on his lap.

Black was harder than Chinese arithmetic and London knew that if she moved her body the right way, she could have him enter her in one single move. At any moment he was going to enter her and there would be no turning back once they went down the road they traveled.

"What's wrong?" he asked with a frown plastered across his face.

Noticing the look, she smiled and nudged his face. "Don't hurt me," she said raising her hips. She placed her hand firmly around his dick, feeling the girth of his member as she gently slid down on him, causing her to wince in pain from the initial penetration.

London gasped as she felt all of him enter her, leaning over resting her head in the nook of his neck. Kissing his neck tenderly as she moved her hips creating a rhythm.

"Babbbbyyyyyy," she moaned picking up speed. Black leaned his head back on the pillow, as his hands traveled down her waist grabbing ahold of her as she rode him like a professional jockey.

"I got you," he said. Feeling her tightness wrapped around him, pulling him in and out of her love box with every move she made.

London closed her eyes, picking up her pace as water splashed on the floor. Slowly running her hands up her body, landing on her breasts.

"Babbbbyyyyyy," she moaned. "I'm…. I'm…. omigod."

Black grabbed her hips forcing her to explode on top. He watched as her breathing picked up and settled once she reached her peak, collapsing onto him as her body twitched from her first orgasm in months. London slid to the other end of the tub and watched as Black stood to his feet. He climbed out of the tub and reached for her hand. London stepped out of the tub, and Black lifted her off the floor sitting her on the bathroom counter.

London's legs wrapped around him as he entered her, causing her to shudder.

"Tell me it's mine," he said as he began gently pounding into her.

London closed her eyes enjoying the ride that Black was taking her on.

"Tell me," he whispered in her ear.

"Bllllllaaaccccckkkkk," she moaned. "Babbbbyyyyyy."

Black seemed to hit every spot that London had and a few that she didn't know existed.

"Tell me," he said as he gently bit her neck

"Ohmygod it's yours," she moaned.

Black had pumped in and out of her in a slow and steady pace, making sure to open her walls just enough so that he could really give her what she needed.

"I can't take it," she said as tears threatened to run down her cheeks.

"You can," he said. Black pulled out of her and turned her over.

London looked at him through the mirror and smirked placing one of her legs on the counter and arching her back perfectly. Black looked at her reflection and locked eyes with her. Placing his dick at her entrance, he entered her. Both seemed to moan at the same time. Grabbing a handful of her hair he yanked her head back, sloppily kissing her never stopping as he fucked her like a man on a mission. London tried to throw her ass back but every time she did Black would match her rhythm causing her to think that he was going to break something.

"Daddyyyyyyyy," she moaned. "Black babbbbyyyyy"

Black grabbed ahold of her hips and went for what he knew. He gave London everything that he had and being that he had waited three months to sleep with her he was going to show her what she had been missing. Feeling himself about to bust he pulled out releasing his hot load onto her ass cheeks.

Leaning against the wall trying to catch his breath, he watched as London took her leg down from the counter and placed her arms folded laying her head atop them.

"What happens now?" she asked.

Black didn't answer her, he walked over towards the custom-built shower turning on the water. He grabbed her arm pulling her close to him and kissed her.

"Whatever you want," he replied.

Black led London into the shower, where they washed each other's bodies and took their love making to the bed. Their union was officially solidified.

# *Chapter Two*

"Do you think she'll come?" Sable asked as she stood in her full-length mirror. Placing a white gold triple row diamond necklace around her neck fastening the clasp, she admired her reflection.

Sable Clark was a woman well into her late fifties but could give a woman half her age a run for their money Her chocolate skin meshing perfectly with the black lace bodysuit, makeup that had been perfectly done, and her auburn colored tresses had been neatly pressed and flowed freely over her shoulders. Standing five foot six, the woman was stacked in all the right places.

Standing in her walk-in closet that was the size of a small apartment, with rows of designer clothes straight from the racks of Neiman Marcus and off the runways of Paris, numerous pairs of pumps, sandals, and boots sat on shelves like modern pieces of art. The closet had been filled with his and her drawers that held undergarments, sleepwear, and clothes that weren't meant to be hung, a display case that had been taken from the show room of

Tiffany's jewelry store which held every piece of jewelry that the couple owned.

Wall to wall plush white carpeting, white painted walls that matched the drawers and shelving of the closet. Portraits of the couple throughout the years placed strategically throughout the room as well as several vases filled with various assortments of fresh cut flowers.

Taking a seat on the white lounge sofa he began slipping into his dress socks. "I don't know," his baritone boomed from behind her.

"I haven't spoken to that child in over two weeks, and you were the last one to see her. Did she mention anything about coming to the party?" Sable asked turning to look at him. "You would think that she would've let us know if she were showing up tonight. She's missed several Christmas's and I would hate for her to miss this one, especially since she's within city limits."

Robert looked at Sable and groaned. True he was the last of the two to see their daughter, but with what happened during their last encounter, Robert could've gone the rest of his life never having contact with the fruit of his loins.

Robert hadn't been given the opportunity to tell Sable what happened at the meeting, thanks to the gossip site that was hell bent on telling their business. So, when the news broke, he gave his wife the watered-down version, never divulging the facts that resulted in London sparing his life that day. No, that was something that he needed to keep to himself.

London had clearly drawn a line in the center of the Earth letting him know, that him walking away that night was a courtesy and she was indeed going to take care of him when the time came. Robert couldn't turn mother against daughter, and although the bond and love that he and his daughter once shared had all been wiped away he couldn't fathom that for Sable, and London had made it abundantly clear that blood was no match for a woman with a crew of able bodied killers at her disposal.

"I don't know. I haven't spoken to her in a few days, and the last time I saw her we didn't get around to talking about the party," he said truthfully.

Sable sighed as she walked over towards him, handing him the diamond tennis bracelet and extending her wrist. "I hope she does come. It'll be nice to have the whole family together again."

Robert fastened the clasp and tapped her wrist. "The whole family won't be here," he said coldly.

Forty years of friendship, brotherhood, and family had all been wiped away. While he knew that holding the annual Christmas Eve party had been tradition, he didn't feel up for partying. Robert wanted to mourn the deaths of his comrades, but he had to put on a brave face and go on as if spending the first holiday without the men he had come up with didn't bother him.

"Well I'll call her and see if she has plans for this evening," Sable said heading back towards the mirror.

Looking at Robert's reflection in the mirror, placing a smile onto her face. After thirty years of marriage Robert was still the man of life, and she had loved him more than she had on the day the two had married. Robert's smooth chestnut complexion, his muscular build that even in his old age he continued to keep toned, staggering at six feet four inches in height, his gray goatee and Caesar cut had always been groomed to perfection giving him a more distinguished look, and wired gold frames covered his big brown eyes.

For as much as Sable loved him and being that there wasn't a thing in the world that she wouldn't do for him she knew that there were something's she couldn't come between, and from the moment she had mentioned her name she knew that his relationship with their daughter was a fight she didn't have a dog in.

The moment the vote was cast giving Black and London full reign over the family, Robert had tried everything he could to make sure his presence was still felt. He couldn't grasp that he was no longer the boss of the family and refused to find an outlet to unload the free time that he now had. Instead he opted for running several of the charters of the Royal's behind the new King and Queen's back. While Sable didn't agree with his tactic's she knew better than to say anything to him. Her role as Queen of the Royals had been fulfilled, and now she looked forward to the days of social events and spending time with friends that weren't apart of a criminal enterprise.

"You do that," he said standing to his feet. Walking over to the counter space grabbing the pair of black Armani slacks stepping into them. "Just make sure that if she comes here, she shows respect. I don't want none of that street shit in here tonight."

Sable rolled her eyes. "Do I want to know?" she asked looking at him and placing her hands on her hips. "Whatever is going on between the two of you I suggest you fix it, tonight."

Robert mumbled under his breath as he tucked his undershirt into his pants, while Sable walked out of the closet. Walking towards the desk that sat in the far corner of the room, she moved the stack of envelopes that sat on top of her cellphone. Scrolling through the contacts stopping on London's number, running her fingers threw her hair as the line trilled in her ear.

Rrrrrrrinnnng. Rrrrrrrrinnnng. Rrrrrrrrinnnng.

"Hello," London's voice came onto the line. Her soft voice was just above a whisper, and held groggy undertones giving Sable the impression that she was asleep.

"London, it's you mother," she said into the phone.

"I know mom," she said irritated. "What's going on?"

Sable looked at the clock that hung on the wall and shook her head. "We were wondering if you were coming to the Christmas Eve party tonight."

London cleared her throat, "I didn't have any plans on coming out."

Sable's heart sank. She didn't know that things between them had caused her family to become so far removed from each other's lives that her daughter would miss the most important event of the year. Christmas was the time that they were to put their differences to the side and come together as a family.

"I would like if you would come tonight," Sable said almost in a pleading tone. "It'll be nice to have you here. Your aunts, uncles, and cousins are all coming up. It'll be good for everyone to see you."

"I don't know mom," she said. "I haven't spoken with your husband since the last meeting and I doubt that he wants to see me right now."

Sable sighed and took a seat in the chair. "London," she started as Robert walked into the room holding his cufflinks. Sable quickly buttoned his cufflinks and shooed him away. "Everything will be fine. If you're not doing anything tonight, try to come by."

"Sure, mom we'll try to make it," she said.

"Who's we?"

"Oh, dad didn't tell you," London said in a sarcastic tone. "There's a new Board and I would love for the both of you to meet them. So, if I come, they come."

Sable stood to her feet and walked into the closet. She snapped her fingers drawing his gaze to her.

'What happened at that meeting?' she mouthed.

Robert scuffed as he continued going about the business of getting dressed. Sable sighed rolling her eyes at his back. She walked over towards her jewelry counter and leaned against it, shaking her head as she looked down at her nails.

"If bringing the members of the Board will make you feel secure then they are more than welcome here," Sable responded knowing that she needed to find a medium to get her family in the same room.

London chuckled "Alright, but let Stone know that I'll be calling a meeting at midnight. The West Wing of the house would do just fine," she said into the phone before ending the call.

Sable placed the phone on the display case and turned her attention to Robert. She needed to know what transpired at the last meeting, and why her husband had been the only Original to make it out alive.

---

London sat up in the bed and looked over at the man who was sound asleep. Glancing over at the digital clock on the nightstand next to him which red illuminated numbers read, 7:48 PM, as she leaned against the headboard.

Since the night the two first made love, London had all but formally moved into his house. After discussing what they assumed to be true about Sade, London and the girls had made it abundantly clear that staying at the hotel was no longer an option. So, it didn't bother her as much when Black sent someone to the Ritz Carlton to retrieve her belongings.

Black had made it clear that he didn't want London to leave. He liked the idea of having someone to come home to after spending his day in the streets and being that she was the only one who would understand the street politics that surrounded the Family, he needed London there to sort out his thoughts.  London continued to run her business all from the confines of Black's house, and after taking a week vacation in addition to the holiday she had more time to explore the newfound relationship between her and Black.

"What?" he said in a groggy tone never opening his eyes.

"You want to go out?" she asked stretching her arms above her head. "My parents are having their Christmas party tonight."

Black opened one eye and looked at her. The tousled state that her hair was in due to the constant pulling and yanking that her tresses had endured during their marathon sex session made her look like a mad woman, her naked body partially covered by the sheet, and yet to him she was still the most beautiful creature he had ever met.

"You want to go?" he asked climbing out of the bed. London watched as he walked towards the bathroom, closing the door behind him.

Running her hands aimlessly over her hair thinking of the worst-case scenario if they did go to the party. Knowing that her mother hadn't been fully aware of what she had said to her father during their last encounter caused her to smile. She had to admire her father for keeping that tidbit to himself.

Black walked out of the bathroom and looked at her. Unaware that he was in the doorway, he watched the devilish smirk that was written across her face. Whatever was brewing behind her smile he didn't need to know the details he was willing to ride through it all with her. No questions ever needed to be asked.

"We going?" he asked walking over towards the bed. Sliding next to her, pulling her close to him gently kissing her shoulder.

She shrugged. "It'll be the first time I would be seeing my dad since the meeting."

"And the first time that nigga is alone," he added.

London shook her head as thoughts of the betrayal of the members came flooding back to her. Many of them she had grown up knowing most of her life, majority she had considered uncles- family. She knew that the hit would affect her father the most, but there were still underlying tensions between the two. Issues that she hadn't offered to tell Black nor anyone else in the Family.

But if she were going to be in the same room as him, she knew there was nothing to stop either of them from exploding onto the next.

# *Chapter Three*

Holidays had always been the worst time of the year for him, and as he drove down the mile-long driveway leading to the estate the disdain he had for the holiday seemed to leave the moment he saw the house.

Rick Ross's song John Doe pumped through the speakers of his Range Rover, with enough bass and treble that it shook the windows of the cars he passed along the way.

Black looked out the tinted window of the car in amazement. The manicured lawn was covered with biodegradable artificial snow that surrounded a Christmas tree which would've put the one that sat at Rockefeller Center to shame, it had been decorated with oversized bulbs, ribbons, and strung with white lights that flickered to the sounds of carols, with large boxes wrapped in colorful paper resembling presents.

The entire estate had been decorated beautifully, with numerous lights, tinsel, and wreaths hanging about, reminding him and his crew of the houses they would only see in movies.

Foreign and domestic cars lined the side of the driveway, no longer were there members of the security that covered the grounds escorting people to the house like he had seen on his first visit.

Black took a deep pull from his blunt as they rode pass members of what he could only assume were people from London and Karma's family as he pulled his car towards the front of the house, heading for the makeshift valet station that sat in the middle of the driveway with several men dressed in red vests who greeted drivers, and disappeared to carry out their task.

"I knew Stone was paid cuz," Face said from the passenger seat. "But this shit. This nigga must got money coming out the ass."

Black exhaled the smoke from his lungs and shook his head. "He does," he said looking in the rearview mirror at the car that trailed his.

"You sure this shit is just family," Vine said from the backseat. "It's hella mothafucka's up in here."

"London said that only her actual family was invited to Christmas Eve dinner. So, to answer your question, yeah, it's only the family," Black said placing the blunt that he was smoking in the ashtray.

"What's the plan when we go up in here?" Vine asked.

Black shrugged. "It's the London show. I don't know what baby got planned but I know it's something."

"It got to be," Face responded. "Got our asses out here dressed like pallbearers and shit. So, whatever it is. It better be worth it."

Black was the only child born to his parents. His mother worked as hard as she could to raise her son after his father had died when he was only six. His mother worked multiple jobs just to put food on the table, and she tried her best to raise her son to become something other than a product of their environment. With all his mother's efforts he still turned out to become what she feared.

Black's cousins Face and Vine were only a few months older than he was and had managed to turn the once quiet child into a ruthless street nigga. It was rumored that all of the Harrison boys had a little devil in them, but it wasn't until they were older and Black had developed his craft that everyone soon realized that Black was the devil reincarnate, and Face and Vine were his disciples that would do his bidding with no questions asked.

"Fucking around with London ass it might be a funeral," Vine capped as he opened the car door.

"Just know if shit does go left in here tonight protect London," Black said seriously.

Face looked at Black with a perplexed look on his face. "You really think Stone gon' try some shit tonight?"

"I don't know," he said as the valet walked towards his door. "But if that nigga does, we are ending all this shit tonight."

"You know something that we don't," Vine capped.

Black sighed. "London thinks that Stone is behind the whole Senate thing, and she wants that nigga dead. But, she doesn't wanna be the one to pull the trigger."

Opening the car door, he adjusted his suit jacket. Handing his car keys to the valet he stepped around to where Vine and Face stood looking towards the door. The woman's shape was a silhouette from the dimly lit lights that danced in the background coming from the house. He watched as she greeted her guests with a hug and motioned for them to enter the house. A grin crossed his face, and he could feel his boys looking at him.

"Who she thinks gon do the job?" Face asked.

Black pointed towards the front door of the house and nodded. "Her."

---

Stepping from the car as the valet opened their doors, Karma, Raven, and London walked towards the men. London had opted for riding with her girls because she needed to give them the game plan for the evening. Although it was a family event, there was still business that needed to be tended to and she wasn't going to let anything go undone. She had already made the decision that her father was a loose end, and one thing she knew for certain. She couldn't have any loose ends this late in the game.

Placing a call to both of her girls less than two hours ago letting them know that she was indeed going to the Christmas party and she needed them to go with her.

Karma had already decided that she was going long before London had asked her to accompany her, and Raven never asked a question, she was just happy to get out of the house for a few hours. Raven's trip to Chicago had been canceled leaving her in the city, and she didn't want to be alone. It was the first Christmas in a long list of those to come where she wouldn't be able to make it home, and she was feeling the effects.

London walked over towards Black and stepped into his embrace. The smell of his cologne mixed with weed filled her nostrils, as she began adjusting his tie. The two hours that London had given each of them to pull themselves together wasn't much, but they had all managed to be dressed to the nines. The girls had all chosen to wear black evening gowns that clung to their curves and flowed freely over the ground.

Karma's hourglass frame hugged the fabric of the black floor length Mac Duggal dress, the lace fabric displaying her butter pecan complexion with feathers lining the sleeves and bottom of the gown. Her hair had been freshly done into a bob cut with blonde streaks cascading through the strands.

Raven was dressed in a mermaid cut dress, with the back of the dress dipping low with crystals and pearls lining the cut of the dress and stopping just above where her ass began. Her long brown tresses had been pulled into a neat up-do resembling something from the roaring 20's era and displaying the three carat diamond studs and matching necklace she wore.

London opted for an off the shoulder mermaid cut dress that cut low between her breasts. Her auburn colored tresses had been straightened dancing down her shoulders, a diamond and emerald necklace donned her neck, with matching earrings, and bracelet.

As she looked over at the men who had traded in thug attire for suits and ties, with polished shoes she couldn't help but smile. Wrapping her arms around his neck she kissed him lightly and wiped the gloss she had transferred from her to him.

"So, this is the castle that held you hostage all those years?" Face said looking London over.

"Yeah," she smirked. "This is it."

"How much you think a house like this would set a nigga like me back?"

"Trust me you wouldn't want this much house even if you had the chance," London said. Directing her attention back to Black.

"You sure you wanna do this?" Black asked looking at her. Running his hands up and down over her arms as the chill bumps took over her skin that was bare trying to transfer heat.

London had taken the liberty of filling Black in on every detail that happened at the meeting, leaving out the words she had spoken to her father the last time they had saw one another. Expecting Black to disagree with her and her movements, she braced for the worse. But when he let her know that whatever she wanted to do was good for him, knowing that she wouldn't put them in any situation that would cause any member of the Royal's harm.

"Looks like we don't have much of a choice now," she said looking at the door.

Black's gaze followed hers as they both watched the couple step out onto the front porch. Sable and Stone stood holding hands in a fashion that reminded onlookers of the Obama's standing on the white house stairs, waving at guests. London looked at her crew and then back towards her parents.

"Let's do this," she said interlocking her fingers with Black's.

# *Chapter Four*

Standing at the top of the stairs overlooking the people who gathered below, Robert watched as members of his family danced, drank, and conversed as if they didn't have a care in the world. For many of them they didn't, but for those that were members of the Royal's, like Robert they were feeling the impact of not having those whom they considered family around this holiday season. It was the first time in the past few days that he felt alone, and even with his house filled with people the emptiness that weighed his soul was unbearable.

In the life he lived he knew that nothing lasts forever, and that death was a constant in the business, it was the unwritten role buried in the job description that each member knew would come but no one not even him knew that it would come from the one person he loved more than anyone else, London.

He and his wife had tried to give London the best of everything. Private schools, tutors, shopping sprees, and funding the life she had become accustomed to until she was well into her twenties. They'd raised their daughter in the lap of luxury, giving her enough tools to compete with the upper echelon of the world, a far cry from the ghettos of the South-Central streets they'd come from. Sheltering her in the Bel-Air neighborhood, shielding her from the ills of the world he had created, only to hand deliver her to that very world. Unknowingly unlocking the door to hell that dwelled within her soul.

Robert loved his daughter more than he loved his own life and would've rather died than to have any harm come her way. It had been that way since the first time he had looked into her emerald green eyes.

From the moment she had been voted Queen, he noticed the change in her. It appeared as if London had transformed seemingly overnight into a beast that he no longer knew, and when she'd ordered the deaths of everyone close to him it only confirmed what he knew to be true. No amount of shelter can keep the inner beast contained. You can take a lion out of the jungle and raise it in captivity, but at the end of the day it was still a lion with a thirst for flesh and blood.

Watching as Sable sashayed around the room greeting guests as they entered the house, and making sure that everything was to her specifications, he casually took sips from the Scotch filled glass in his hand that had turned into a watered down mess that no longer held the sting that he needed to mask the pain that he was feeling.

Descending the curved staircase that took him to the first level where the partygoers were, he sat his glass on the tray of a passing waiter and made his way towards his wife. The navy colored Zac Posen mermaid gown she wore clung to her curves as if it were painted on, the five-inch heels she wore had her standing shoulder height to him. Wrapping up the conversation she was having with a distant cousin, she smiled at him and the two walked a short distance. Sable rested her head on his shoulder as the two listened to the carolers sing their renditions of traditional Christmas carols.

Sable had out done herself, per usual. Dancers from the Debbie Allen dance academy performed the Hot Chocolate Nut Cracker in the library for the guests in attendance, several Christmas trees had been placed throughout the house with presents wrapped neatly under each for the people in attendance, servers walked about the lower floor carrying trays of hors d'oeuvres and champagne, a private chef who was busy in the kitchen and dining area preparing the three course meal that Sable had requested.

"I hope she gets here soon. We're about to start dinner," she said turning her attention towards him.

"What happens if she doesn't?"

She sighed, "Robert we've been over this. London is the only child that we have and its very imperative that she spends the holidays with her family."

"London's a grown woman," he said looking at her. "If she comes fine. If not, then to hell with it."

"You say that as if you don't want to see her," she said.

"It's not that I don't want her here," he admitted. Grabbing a drink from a passing waiter. "There's some things you can't come back from, and what she did the other day is one of those things."

Sable looked up and frowned. "Unless you're ready to tell me what exactly happened at the meeting and not that watered-down bullshit that you keep trying to push, then I really don't want to hear this right now," she said and walked away.

Robert stood there watching as she headed towards the door. A part of him knew that he should've told her everything that went on at the meeting, but to him it was more than enough information on the gossip site, and he felt there wasn't a need to divulge any more details.

Noticing one of his cousins coming his way, Robert made a beeline behind Sable. He walked onto the front porch and stood next to her. The winter nights air hadn't been as forgiving as the day, bringing with it a cold front that made him pull tightly on the Armani jacket that he was wearing. Stepping over towards his wife, he looked down the few stairs and watched the six individuals who had congregated at the bottom.

Sable unconsciously grabbed his hand, interlocking her fingers with his as they watched London climb the stairs. She was beautiful, just as beautiful as her mother.

'Don't start no shit unless they do,' he said to himself. Sable had let go of his hand and walked over towards their daughter, embracing her and her guests in hugs and kisses. She took a step back and turned towards him with a smile plastered across her face.

Robert knew that Sable was as happy as she'd ever been now that London was finally home to spend what he knew would be their last holiday together and forced a smile onto his face. He walked over towards the group and shook hands with the men, and hugged Karma and Raven. When he turned to face London, a lump formed in his throat.

He didn't know whether to hug her, shake her hand or simply let her be.

Turning towards Black he looked him over and smirked. "I heard y'all wanna talk business."

"Naw," he said nodding his head slightly towards London. "London wanted to talk. I'm just here as an arm piece."

Robert looked at his daughter and nodded in her direction. London feeling his discomfort stepped forward and wrapped her arms around him, pulling him into a hug.

"Let's talk," she whispered in his ear.

Robert closed his eyes briefly as he released her. London stepped past him and headed into the house with her crew behind her.

---

Walking into the house she was immediately greeted by the warmth that filled the home. The house had been decorated beautifully and looked like winter wonderland had thrown up all its magic into the house. Family members filled every section, and as she waved to the familiar faces in the crowd, she grabbed Black's arm sliding his jacket sleeves up slightly to look at the hands of the Movado watch that he was wearing. Seeing that it was almost midnight, she headed towards the west wing of the house, with the rest of her entourage behind her.

Pushing through the heavy wood double doors that separated the west wing from the rest of the house, she walked down the corridor towards the steel enforced door, stopping she turned and looked at her parents.

"Is the code still my birthday?" she asked in a soft tone that seemed to echo throughout the empty space.

Her father nodded and watched as she pressed the numbers into the keypad. Taking a step back as the doors made a loud clanking sound before sliding to the left and opening.

The motion censored lights came on once she stepped into the room. Looking around the room, London grimaced. The room had been painted a maroon color that matched the mahogany wood floors, a conference table that seated twenty sat in the middle of the room with oversized plush chairs surrounding them and a hand carved box that held her father's favorite cigars, the north facing wall had been filled with monitors that displayed every square inch of the home, a large bar sat in the corner of the room stocked with every brown liquor imaginable. Other than several oil paintings that hung on the walls the room hadn't been as decorated as the rest of the house, and London understood why.

London had only been in the room a few times in her life, it was her father's war room, and had been completely off limits to her mother and herself. It was the only room in the house where members of the Board were able to speak freely and discuss business. The room wasn't monitored like the rest of the house by cameras, and her father had paid quite the pretty penny to have the room installed with a device that killed any transmitters in case anyone entered the room with a wire.

She motioned for her friends to have a seat and walked around the table taking a seat at the head. Karma and Raven had sat to her left, and Black, Vine, and Face had taken the seats to her right. London watched as her mother pressed a button on the wall closing the door, and both of her parents sat on the opposite end of the table.

"Say your peace," her father spoke. He was looking at Black, but he directed his words to London. From the hug that he had given her she knew that her father was uneasy looking at her, and he didn't want to say so.

"Do you think I see you as an enemy?" London asked.

"Do you?" he retorted.

London shrugged and looked at Black. "I don't know yet," she answered truthfully. "Did you tie up those loose ends?"

"What loose ends?" Sable asked. She looked at everyone sitting around the table, landing on London.

"I told him to tie up whatever loose ends he had." London said never taking her eyes off her father.

"What's going on?" Sable asked. "Black? Karma?"

Black shrugged. "It's between them."

Karma didn't say a word. She couldn't. Her loyalty was to London, and it wasn't her place to say a thing.

Sable looked at Robert. Placing one of her hands on the top of his and using the other to turn his face towards her. "What's going on between you two? Is this about the meeting?"

"You want to tell her, or should I?" London asked.

Robert looked at Sable and shook his head. "It's about the Senate."

"What about the Senate?" Sable asked confused.

"Why didn't you tell anyone that you were the one who started the Senate?" she said looking at him. She watched as his eyebrows connected and he looked over at Sable.

The look that was on her face was of total confusion. It was at that moment that London knew that her father hadn't told her why she had the members of the Board killed.

"For over forty years you've ran the Royal's," London continued looking at him. "Forty years that you built a life and business that you intended to pass down, and not once did you think to tell any of us that you were also the one who created the enemy that you had your family trying to eliminate."

"You don't know what you're talking about," he said looking from Sable to her.

"You're saying that, you had no idea who the Senate was?" Black chimed in looking at him.

Robert looked at him and frowned. "Everyone with their ears to the streets knows who the Senate is," he snapped.

"And anyone with their ear to the streets knows that the Senate sprung up out of nowhere and on the strength of your word we believed that these niggas was the enemy," Vine said. "We've been going to war with niggas that were playing both sides, and you didn't think that anyone would find out, and you didn't think to let anyone know either."

"I just want to know why'd you start them," London said. "You already had the Royal's what was the purpose of starting the Senate. Did you get a kick out of having your own crews wipe each other out? Having everyone believe that we're into it with niggas from the other side, and the whole time you and your fucked-up ass Board is around here playing puppet master."

Robert gave London a look that if looks could kill, she would've been dead. He hadn't raised her to be defiant, at least not to him. He hadn't raised London to talk to him in such a manner, and here she was questioning his authority. Making him look like a weakling in his house.

"London," Sable said in a low tone. "The members of the Board were the Senate?"

She watched as her father gave her mother a look that spoke volumes. Feeling herself, London decided to add to the flames of the already smoldering fire.

"Yes," London said and smirked. "He didn't tell you."

She didn't say a word as she stood from the chair she was in and walked towards the door. Before the doors could open completely Sable had exited the room.

London wanted to run after her, but she knew that her mother needed this moment. She needed her to carry out the plan that she had played over and over in her mind, since she had decided to come to the party.

Running her hand through her head she smiled and looked around the table. "Being that you went against the request I made. Is there anything that you would like to say?"

Robert sat back in his seat and shrugged. "No. There's no need."

London chuckled. "Your wife just found out that you created the Senate. The very Senate that killed her brother twenty years ago, and you didn't think that you needed to tie up any lose ends on your part."

Robert swallowed hard. "I didn't pull the trigger."

"And you didn't kill the mothafucka's who killed her brother. Instead you ate from the same plate, drank from the same cup, and I'm willing to bet my future that you had those same niggas running in and out of this house. All under your wife's nose, never once telling her that you were behind the hit," London said standing to her feet.

"London," Karma said just above a whisper. "What's going on?"

London ignored her as she walked towards the middle of the table removing two cigars. Cutting off the tips she threw one on the table for her father and took the gold lighter from the box lighting hers before tossing him the lighter as well.

Taking in a deep pull and exhaling a cloud of smoke, London walked back over to her seat and sat down. She looked at her father and shook her head.

"Everything that you do from this moment forward will have consequences," he said grabbing the cigar and lighting it. "You think that you're playing the game and winning. You will never beat me."

London shrugged, "Maybe I will, maybe I won't. But I know one thing."

"What's that?"

"Everyone my mother has is in this house, and for twenty years they've all been trying to unlock the mystery of who killed their brother. She knew that the line of the Senate was bullshit and now," she paused for dramatic effect. "She thinks that you had something to do with her brothers murder."

The two became locked in a stare down. It was as if no one else were in the room with the two as they silently watched one another to see who was going to make the next move. London didn't know what her father was thinking, but if she had to guess at that moment, he regretted the day he nutted in her mother.

Robert sighed, as he took in a deep pull from his cigar. "We were moving so much shit that I needed another team to move more. They were just giving us the shit. We were already supplying all of California and half of Nevada, but there was more coming in. Every damn day."

"So," Black started. "You supplied the Senate and had both sides going against the grain for what."

"That shit was happening already," he said waving him off. "The Crips and Bloods were never going to get along, and the drug game just-"

"Just made it easier for you to create an organization that killed more niggas from my hood than any other gang," Vine said becoming aggravated.

"Man, them niggas was going to die regardless," he said matching Vine's tone.

Black, Vine and Face all stood their feet and looked at Robert. Black's jaw muscles began flexing a clear indication that he was pissed, and the others were waiting on Robert to make a move. They didn't need much, but it would've been better for Robert to give them any reason to think that he was reaching for anything, giving them enough reason to pull the guns that were tucked in their waistbands.

"Not now y'all," London said to the men. "We're not the ones who's going to do it for him. That'll be too easy. He expects that."

The men looked at London and then towards Robert. She didn't need this shit, not now. There was a plan in motion, and they weren't going to fuck it up, by having a pissing contest.

"It's gotten back to me that you've been working in some of the charters," London said looking at him. "I did you a favor by letting you walk out of that meeting, and this is the thanks I get."

"You don't do me no fucking favors," he seethed.

London chuckled, "Oh, but I do. Who do you think told me that there was a meeting called in the first place? Them niggas loyalty to you went out the window the moment the votes were cast."

Robert took a deep pull from the cigar and looked across the table at her. "I don't give a fuck. This is my family, I built this shit," he said his voice booming throughout the room. "I still run this shit."

"You were out," London snapped. "You were fucking out. You could've gone the rest of your life knowing that you built something that's going to last forever. What more did you want? What more did you need?"

"You're never out. You can wipe the board clean and start a new game, but at the end of the day. It's always the same game, and even if the players do change. The old ones are still playing, so you're never really out," he said with a chuckle. "In the game, the only way out is in a bag."

"Robert," Sable said her voice low and shaky.

No one in the room had noticed that she had entered the room, and as they looked at the nine-millimeter she held in her hands all eyes fell on the woman standing next to the steel doors.

"Did you kill Trey? Did you have my brother killed?" she asked as she pointed the gun at him.

Sable looked around the room, locking eyes with everyone that was seated, and then placed her sights back on her husband. She thought about her late brother, and the horrible fate he had suffered twenty years ago. Murdered in broad daylight, while waiting at a red light. The police summed the case up as a wrong place wrong time scenario and closed the case as quickly as it were opened.

When the rumors started circulating that the Senate had been behind his murder, Robert had swore to her that he'd have the men murdered. Now she knew why she had never heard of their fate.

"I don't know what you're talking about," Robert said looking at her.

"What the fuck is going on?" Raven whispered.

London nodded towards her parents. "You'll see."

Sable flicked the safety off, and  pulled back on the hammer pointing the gun towards Robert. "I've always known when you were lying," Sable said shaking her head.

"All you mothafucka's get out of my house," Robert yelled.

London laughed, "He still thinks he's in control."

"Obviously," Black agreed.

Boom... Boom... Boom.

The shots that rang in the room caused everyone to jump. London looked over and noticed that her mother's finger was on the trigger. Sable shot three shots into the ground next to Robert's seat causing him to look at her.

As tears streamed down her cheeks. "Did you kill my brother?"

"Yes, I had that nigga killed," he snapped looking at her. "He wasn't shit but a fucking pawn. He was disposable."

London stood to her feet and threw the cigar in the middle of the table.

"Let's go," she said to her crew.

She watched as the people she had walked into the room with left out, grabbing Karma's hand turning her slightly so that they locked eyes. Running her hands down her gown, she walked over towards her parents. She looked down at her father and leaned over kissing his cheek.

"I love you daddy. But your time is up," she said before turning to look at her mother.

The two women looked one another over, and as London fought back the tears from falling, she wiped away at the ones that flowed freely down her mother's cheeks.

London had known that if she had given her mother the information she needed about who actually killed her brother, she'd handle the situation herself. She also knew that her parents loved each other more than they loved themselves, and after tonight she'd learn just how far their love went.

As a lump formed in her throat, London just stared at her mother unable to speak. Sable placed her free hand on her daughter's cheek and kissed her lightly on the forehead.

"I know," Sable said looking at her. London walked out of the room and stood in the hallway.

"You knew how much it hurt me when I found out he died," Sable could be heard. "You knew how many nights I cried because he was gone, and you…you were behind the whole thing."

Robert adjusted the suit jacket and looked at her. He had loved Sable for as long as he had been alive, knowing that he was going to die at the hands of the woman he had vowed to love, honor, and protect he took one last pull of the cigar before tossing it on the table. Watching as its embers danced atop the wood table.

"I love you. Both of you," he said loud enough for London to hear.

"I know and I love you too," Sable replied.

Boom…Boom…Boom…

The shots rang throughout the corridor as the group walked through the double doors that lead to the rest of the house. London stopped, trying to hold back the tears that were starting to form.

Boom…

As she heard the loud thud of the body hit the ground. She turned and looked at her mother's legs as they lay on the floor of the room.

Fighting to hold back the tears from falling, she placed her hand on the door and stepped into the rest of the house. Black placed his hand on the small of her back as they made their way outside.

No one said a word as they all knew what happened. Robert and Sable had gone out as they had lived, together. London walked down the stairs and waited in silence for Karma's car to be brought around by the valet. She looked at her girls and then towards Black.

"What happens now?" Karma asked in a low tone.

London looked at her. "We find the bitch that's responsible for that site," she said. "And we continue to go about our business."

"What about them?" Karma said pointing towards the house.

London shrugged. "The funeral will be held next week. Wear white," she stated in an even tone.

The valet parked the car directly in front of them and London stepped into the passenger seat. They each looked at her as if she had completely lost her mind, because indeed she had.

London was no longer held by the bondage of what her parents expected of her nor what the streets painted the Queen to be. London had just claimed her place at the top of the ghetto food chain and come hell or high water she was never coming down.

Karma climbed into the car and drove off as the first of many screams escaped the house as partygoers discovered the couple who lay dead in the west wing of the house.

## 2016

# *Chapter Five*

*Good morning my city slickers, this is Los Angeles Confidential the one and only source into the scandalous lives of the Royal's. It's been six months since the fall of the old regime, and with the King and Queen still in hiding, we're beginning to wonder if the Royal's like the Senate has fallen off the map. Ready or not, you can't hide. London and Black, where are you? Come out, come out wherever you are. You'll soon hate me, L.A. Confidential.*

As London looked down at her cell phone, she couldn't help but to feel annoyed. Over the past few months, she had spent more than a few thousand dollars to get the gossip site removed from the internet, but to no avail. The programmers that she'd hired couldn't track down the location of the original site, giving London nothing to go on. With emails coming in daily, taunting her to come out of what they considered hiding, she was more determined than ever to locate the site's originator. She was totally engulfed in the email that had come in that morning, knowing that there were a series of others that were soon to follow.

It had been six months since what was dubbed as the bloodiest holiday season in The Royals history. London had spent the past few months getting back into the swing of things at work, being that she had neglected work almost entirely. In addition to London ruling over the Royal's she was the sole proprietor of, Clark & Associates, an investment firm that catered to many, but her main clients were members of the Royal's and those that carried serious ties to them. Governors, Mayors, Judges, Police Chiefs all had their assets managed, and in many cases hidden with the help of her firm.

Sitting at the conference table surrounded by her employees, as they went over the budget for the quarter, she half listened to Monte, the head of accounting as he finished his presentation.

"If you'll turn to page eight, you'll see that I've taken the liberty to include the next quarters trajectory as well," he said looking around the room. "If we continue to bring in the revenue that we've been seeing over the past two quarters, then Clark & Associates will definitely be on the lips of everyone very soon, and we'll have even more clients that are willing to trust us to invest their dividends."

London looked down at the stack of papers in front of her, shaking her head as she noticed the numbers that were in red ink.

"Thank you, Monte, for your presentation," she spoke in a low tone. "I know that over the past few months I've really been leaning on this team to pretty much run the day to day, and I want you all to know that I am truly grateful. Without you guys Clark & Associates wouldn't have made it past the first quarter. You guys are truly amazing."

The room became filled with pleasantries as London stood to her feet and looked at every member that sat around the twenty-seat conference table, and their assistants who'd stood against the glass walls. Running her hands over the cream-colored pants suit she was wearing, brushing off invisible lint and smoothing wrinkles, she looked down at the last page of the stack and smiled.

"Clark & Associates managed to rake in more than ten million dollars last quarter," she said with a smile on her face.

The room exploded with claps and she raised her hand signaling for them to quiet down. "Many of you don't know that when I started this company, I had no idea what it was that I was doing, but you guys stuck with me through it all, and for that reason alone," she paused for dramatic effect. "I'm giving everyone a bonus at the end of this quarter."

The room once again erupted into a fit of claps and cheers. London smiled as she looked around the room. If there was one thing London had learned over the past few months, feed your team or else you'll end up with a mutiny on your hands.

Although London had all her employees sign non-disclosure agreements to protect the privacy of those who trusted her company to handle their finances, she also placed a non-compete clause in their contracts. Being that any of her employees couldn't violate the non-disclosure agreements was one thing, but she needed them to understand that if they left the firm for any reason, their career as an investor would be over. Each employee had given London the complete control over their livelihoods.

No one that worked in the firm knew of London's life outside of the office. To them she was just another rich girl, who'd managed to use daddy's money and connections to build a life for herself and based on that assumption alone, they were right.

London had used her father's connections to make a life for herself, and his dealings with the Royal's made London a very wealthy woman both legally and illegally. Although she wouldn't dare admit it, she was grateful for the life she lived, and for the world that had been passed down to her.

"London," her assistant Thomas's voice came over the intercom. "There's a call on line two from Mr. Harrison, would you like me to take a message."

London pressed her perfectly manicured finger on the talk button, "No. I'll get it in my office."

The line disconnected, and London began gathering her belongings from the table.

"I believe that was all that was on the agenda for today. Thank you, guys, for coming to this meeting and please," she said turning her attention towards the assistants were standing along the walls. "Don't forget that everyone is a valued member of this organization. I didn't forget about you guys. Monte, I want to set up a meeting after lunch to go over raises for every assistant in this office."

"Yes Ms. Clark," Monte said.

London walked out of the room and headed towards her office. Taking off the five-inch heels that were on her feet, she walked over towards her desk. Placing the stack of papers and her cell on top she grabbed the receiver from the office phone.

"Hey," she said into the phone.

"Took you long enough," the deep baritone boomed through the phone.

"I didn't know I needed to rush, Mr. I'm going to sleep until noon," she said taking a seat in the oversized leather swivel chair.

"You working hard or barely working?"

"I was in a meeting with the staff," she replied.

"Ok," he said and got quiet.

London couldn't remember the last time Black had called her at the office. Whenever he needed her he always sent a text, or called her cellphone, and now that it dawned on her that she was on her office line she frowned.

"What's wrong?"

"Nothing, I just wanted to talk to you about some shit."

"What's going on?" she asked sitting back in her chair.

"How'd you feel if we threw something for the folks around the way?"

"You called me at work to see how I would feel if we threw a party," she said annoyed.

"Nah I was really calling to see what kind of panties you have on."

London giggled and placed her legs on top of the desk leaning back in her chair.

"Well, they're black, lace-"

"Ms. Clark, your eleven thirty is here," Thomas's voice boomed through the intercom.

London frowned and pressed the talk button, "I'll be out in a second."

"Saved by the bell," he said with a chuckle.

"Yeah, some of us still have to work," she said adjusting herself. "Anyway, I'll see you later on tonight."

"Aight ma I love you and all that mushy shit."

"Yeah all that mushy shit," she said ending the call.

London reached into her desk, removing a file and placing it on top of the desk. Walking over to the door, she placed the heels back on her feet, adjusting her clothes, hair, and face she stepped out of the office.

As she made hurried steps towards the reception area of the suite, her heels tapping lightly against the marbled floor. Stepping over towards the reception desk she looked at Thomas and smiled.

"Where's my eleven thirty?" she asked.

"He's right over there," Thomas said pointing towards the man sitting in one of the white armchairs.

London turned towards where Thomas had pointed, and a smile came to her face. As she looked at the six-foot four-inch mountain of a man, with his chestnut complexion, his short cut was embedded with waves, full lips, and pearly white teeth. Dressed in a well-tailored suit that clung to his bone structure as if it were made only for him.

London walked over towards him and extended her hand.

"Hi, I'm London Clark," she said taking his hand in hers.

"Brandon Tyler," he responded with a smile.

"Nice to meet you Mr. Tyler. If you'll follow me, we'll get started."

---

Black sat on the passenger side of his boy/cousin Face's Cadillac truck smoking a blunt. He'd just been picked up from the barber shop that sat off Western and Exposition. After getting his hair and beard tightened up and shooting the shit with the guys that were inside of the shop, he'd placed a call to Face to come and pick him up.

He'd left his car at the house and opted for riding shotgun with his boy for the remainder of the day. Looking down at the gold Rolex on his wrist as the heads showed twelve, Black shook his head.

Over the past few months Black had become more involved with the streets, although he had been named King of the Royal's he didn't feel the need to fade to the back while everyone around him got all the glory. He was a nigga who liked to call shots and get his hands dirty, and as he stared out the window as Face dipped in and out of the afternoon traffic, he remembered that there was a runner who owed him money.

"Take me to that nigga Bo house," he said as he expelled a cloud of smoke. "That nigga owes me some bread."

Face looked over at him and frowned. "Nigga this aint driving Miss Daisy cuz," he snapped. "You ask a nigga like me."

Black looked at him and the two men burst into laughter. Face's dark brown complexion resembled Black's, they both shared the same big brown eyes, but that's where the similarities ended. Black had a beard that he kept trimmed, and a low Caesar cut that was embedded with waves. Face kept a low taper fade, and neatly trimmed goatee that surrounded his pearly whites, and he also had deep dimples.

"What's this shit I hear about you still fucking that bitch Monica?" Face said looking at Black.

Black shrugged. Every day that his feet hit the pavement, he'd hit the streets. While London was tucked away safely at her downtown office, leaving Black alone giving him free reign to do the shit that most niggas did. Although he had a good woman at home, that didn't stop him from occasionally sliding with his ex, Monica. Black saw it as no big deal, and he hadn't told anyone that he was still sleeping with the woman, but now that Face had brought it up. He knew that either Monica was talking, or the streets were watching.

"That silence right there lets me know that you are," Face said looking over at him. Guiding his car down Century, Face continued to weave in and out of traffic as if he were auditioning for a roll in Fast & Furious.

"I only fuck with her when London is you know," he lied.

Face shook his head. "Don't fuck up what you got fucking with these bird brain ass bitches, they'll love to fuck you, get pregnant, and think they got a meal ticket for the rest of their lives."

"I aint fucking with her like that," Black waved him off. "Besides I always strap up when I'm with the bitch."

"Who buys the condoms?"

"She does."

Face scuffed as he looked at him and shook his head. Black looked over at his boy and frowned. He knew that it was only a matter of time before word got back to London, and he knew that if it did there was no telling what'd she do. Before it ever got to that point Black vowed to cut things off with Monica, he didn't need his lifeline leaving him behind some pussy that's barely worth mentioning.

# *Chapter Six*

Karma looked behind her and smirked as she watched Vine walk into her bathroom. The sounds of the water running in the sink, followed by him coming back into the bedroom and wiping his semen off of her ass that was planted in the air.

Karma stood to her feet and walked into the bathroom turning on the shower. It had been a little over a year since Karma and Vine had started sleeping together, and while both were fine with the arrangement that they'd had, Karma knew that it was only a matter of time before the lines became blurred.

Karma still dated other men from time to time, but the moment her and Vine had gotten together she stopped inviting them over. Vine was the only man who had ever been given a key to her house, and while it was given to him under the guise of emergencies Vine seemed to use the key more often than she did.

Vine had moved some of his clothes into one of the spare bedrooms and placed all of his hygiene and grooming products in the front bathroom. While Karma didn't complain, she did find it odd that he wasn't her man, yet he acted as if he were.

Calling everyday just to "check-in" or to "make sure she's not doing some shit that'll get her fucked up". She loved his attention and aggressive behind, but she was a woman she needed a title if she were going to continue to be at his beck and call.

Karma watched as the steam covered the mirror, taking her hand wiping off the glass she caught the reflection of the man standing behind her. He was busy typing on his cell phone. Feeling her staring at him, Vine looked over towards her and flashed a smile.

"Why you looking at me like that?" he asked throwing his phone on the bed.

"No reason," she said grabbing the bonnet off the counter and placing it on her head. Pulling the glass paneled shower doors open she stepped into the hot water.

There were two types of cleaning that a woman did while showering, one was the quick I have somewhere to be wash, and the second wash which most women performed on a daily basis was the I'm about to get some dick. Karma washed her body as if she had a dick appointment and she were scheduled to make close to a million dollars as long as her ass was washed.

Stepping from the shower she grabbed the plush terry cloth bath robe that hung on the hook and wrapped it around herself.

"You didn't even ask me to wash yo back," Vine said looking at her.

"You could've just come in," she said looking at him. "I've never invited you to shower with me before. Normally you just barge in."

Vine looked at her with a smirk on his face. "Damn, what did I do to you today?"

Karma shrugged and walked over towards the shelf that held her lotions, oils, and perfumes. Grabbing the coconut oil, she began moisturizing her body, never once looking at him.

Vine knew that there was something wrong with Karma, she'd had an attitude since the night before. Vine knew what the issue was, but he wasn't going to be the first to admit what they both knew to be true. Karma wanted something more serious, she deserved something more serious. But Vine was knee deep in the game and having a woman at such a pinnacle point in his life wasn't what he needed.

He was fine with what they had. No strings, no titles, just sex, and chilling from time to time.

Vine was about to say something to her, when his cellphone began vibrating. Grabbing the phone off the bed, he looked down at the name that sprawled across the screen before answering.

"Yeah," he said into the phone. Vine listened for a moment and responded, "Say less, let me take a shower and I'm on my way."

Vine ended the call and looked at Karma. "I got some shit to take care of with the fellas," he said looking at her. "Later on I wanna talk to you about some shit."

Karma didn't stop from rubbing the oil on her skin as she said, "Sure."

Vine scuffed and walked into the bathroom closing the door behind him thinking, it was either time to give Karma what she wanted or cut her loose.

---

By the time Karma had finished getting dress it was close to one thirty, she walked down the stairs of her apartment, waving to some of the residents in her building before walking out of the courtyard.

The two-bedroom apartment that Karma lived in sat smack in the heart the sixties neighborhood, and her ghetto ass loved her building. The young niggas and women who hung out in the courtyard were always looking out for her. She was able to live comfortably, come and go as she pleased without being pressed, and never had to worry about someone running into her place.

She'd paid the apartment owner extra to move into the apartment. At the time the owner had no idea why the woman who wore Gucci and Chanel labels wanted to live in the hood, knowing that if she'd shelled out thousands of dollars on designer threads, she could surely afford to live anywhere else. It wasn't until Karma had moved in that the owner understood what the extra money was for.

Karma had gutted the apartment and had a team of designers come and refurbish the rental to her specifications. The owner was initially pissed, but upon inspection of the unit he was in awe.

The floors had been stripped of its off white carpet and replaced with wood floors, several pillars separated the living room from the dining room and were made from real marble, the bathroom bathtubs had been replaced with jacuzzi tubs standalone showers, and a separate room had been added in each bathroom just for the toilet.

Karma had transformed the second bedroom into a full-size closet that held racks on top of racks of clothing, rows of shoes, and glass cabinets that held all of her bags. The master suite had been set with winter white carpet, an oversized bed that was in the shape of a circle that sat in the middle of the floor, mirrors covered an entire wall as well as the ceilings. The renovations cost her well over a few thousand dollars, but Karma gladly paid to live in the south-central neighborhood.

Karma was a hood chick through and through. While London was content with living anywhere other than the very neighborhoods that she had been set to rule over, Karma found her life complete living in those areas.

Walking towards the black BMW that was parked directly in front of the entrance of the building she reached into her purse removing her keys, silencing the alarm. The stares that she received as she walked by a group of men made her smirk.

'I know I look good,' she thought as she climbed into her car. The leather seat burning the skin of her legs, causing her to jump slightly. Turning the car on she pulled down the visor looking herself over once more.

Dressed in shorts that were cut short enough that they showed off her ass cheeks, a sleeveless white body suit that dipped low enough to show the tops of her breast, white Gucci sandals on her feet. Karma rocked three pair of bamboo earrings ranging from extra-large, down to medium, four gold necklaces wrapped around her neck, as she looked down at her acrylic nails, she knew what her first stop would be. As she put the car in gear, she pealed out of the parking space, causing the tires to burn rubber as she sped down the street.

Grabbing her cellphone out of her bag, she dialed Raven's number and placed the phone on speaker.

Rrrrrrrinnnng. Rrrrrrrrinnnng. Rrrrrrrrinnnng

"What's up?" Raven said into the phone.

"I'm on my way to the nail shop," Karma said as she turned down 67th street heading towards Crenshaw. "You wanna meet me there."

"I went yesterday," she said. "Plus you know I have to prepare myself mentally for this shit London got going on."

Karma laughed, "Oh you mean going out tonight with Sade. Don't even sweat it, you know it's just London's fucked up way of keeping the girl close."

"I wish her ass wouldn't do that. I don't trust her no more," Raven said.

"Neither do I," Karma capped. "But until London or Black gives the word, the bitch is untouchable."

"Yeah I hear that shit," Raven said letting out a groan. "So what's the move for tonight anyway."

Karma smiled as she weaved in and out of traffic. "Apparently after the meeting we're supposed to meet London at her house."

"Oh shit," Raven said. "What the fuck happened now?"

## *Chapter Seven*

Face pulled his car in front of a house on Century boulevard and McKinley Avenue, turning off the ignition both men sat back in their seats and looked at the houses on the block. During the course of the drive over the two had smoked a few blunts and were feeling the effects of the weed.

"You ready or are you too damn high," Face said looking over at Black.

Black chuckled. He reached under the seat and removed a nine-millimeter handgun. Checking the gun making sure that it wasn't on safety, and there was a bullet in the chamber.

"Let's do this," he said moving forward and placing the gun in his waistband.

Both men stepped out of the car and headed towards the front of the house. Face looked around the block, making note of the cars that were parked and the people that were out.

Century was a main street, and although it were the middle of the day, most of the residents weren't home, and the elementary school that was down the street hadn't ended so he knew that if things went left the only witnesses would be the passerby's, and everyone knew their stories wouldn't hold up in court.

Climbing the three stairs, Black towards the door and knocked on the door. The sounds of people moving behind the door could be heard, and as Black and Face looked at one another the door flung open.

"He aint here," the woman said in an annoyed tone. Black looked her up and down with a smirk on his face. The woman was fine.

Dressed in a pair of sleep shorts that left nothing to the imagination, spaghetti strap tank that displayed her nipples through the cloth. As he looked over her five feet seven-inch frame, he licked his lips before flashing a smile. She was the color of freshly pressed penny, and her hair was swept into a messy bun on top of her head, doe shaped hazel eyes, a small button nose, and a mole that sat above her top lip.

"You don't even know who I'm here for," he said looking her over.

"Bo," she said with an attitude. "Don't nobody come here unless they're looking for his ass."

"Where he at?" Face asked looking over the woman.

"I don't know."

Black and Face turned and looked at each other, a devilish grin spread across Face's face. Black stepped to the side, giving Face room to burst into the house. The woman fell backwards as she watched the two men barge into her house closing the door behind them.

"Where's he at?" Face asked looking at her.

"I don't know," she said looking at him. If looks could kill, Face would've been dead right where he stood.

"You know," Face snapped grabbing the woman by her hair.

She let out a scream but was silenced by two slaps to the face. "I'm going to ask again, where's Bo?"

She looked at both men, pleading with her eyes but she couldn't command her mouth to speak. She didn't know who they were or what they wanted but it was evident from the way they moved and spoke that they were not to be fucked with. It was at that moment she had to decide, her life or the life of the man who was hiding in her children's bedroom.

---

London sat across from Brandon going over the investment portfolio that had been created for him, coming to the last page she slid the folder across the desk, and sat back in her chair.

Brandon Tyler was handsome, London had to admit that. Whenever the two locked eyes she felt herself turning away, unable to hold his gaze, because she felt as if she were going to get lost in them.

His deep baritone washed over the room like a melody her soul yearned to hear. It didn't take much pressure for London to find out that Brandon was not only handsome, he was smart, well-traveled, and the complete opposite of everything that London was used to in men.

Brandon had taken it upon himself to let her know who he was. She'd learned that he was the oldest of three children, born and raised in Reseda, one of the surrounding cities, he had paid his way through college and law school, and was now working as a deputy district attorney with plans on running for district attorney in the upcoming election.

She was intrigued by the man sitting across from her, and he'd given her more than enough information about himself than she'd cared to know. London did however want to know more about his business but she knew that she couldn't cross the line that had been drawn the moment he stepped into her office. He was a client, nothing more.

His big hands holding the folder closely, as he flipped through the pages shaking his head slightly just before turning the pages, she smirked.

"Any questions?" she asked.

"Just one," he said placing the folder on the desk. "Can I take you to dinner?"

London smiled and shook her head. "I'm sorry. I can't."

"I didn't mean to be forward," he said sitting back in the chair. "I didn't see a ring, so I assumed you were single."

"Mr. Tyler-"

"Brandon," he said flashing a smile. "Please call me Brandon."

"Brandon," she said looking at him. "I don't date clients."

"You can hand my folder over to one of your colleagues and then you won't have to think of the technicality."

She chuckled, "It wouldn't be a technicality, because technically you'll still be a client of mine."

"How so?" he asked genuinely confused.

"I own the firm," she said in a matter of fact tone.

He was silent for a moment, and then flashed a smile. "Clark," he said as it dawned on him. "London Clark."

Brandon looked the woman over and smirked. In all of his thirty-two years he had never met a woman like her. She was smart, beautiful, and from the looks of things she was successful. He didn't know why, but he was immediately attracted to the woman and he wanted her.

"I guess it really wouldn't matter if I worked with anyone else in the firm, you'd still wouldn't be interested in one dinner," he said smiling displaying his perfect thirty-twos.

"I'm sorry," she said standing to her feet. "It's not you, it's just policy."

Brandon shook his head in agreement. "Well in that case, Ms. Clark. I look forward to seeing more of you, for business purposes."

"Like wise," she said walking around her desk. London walked towards the door opening it. "I'll walk you to the front."

Brandon smiled and walked out of the office. London closed the door, as the two walked towards the front of the suite.

"I'll have one of my associates send over the final paperwork for you to finalize. It shouldn't take more than a few days to completely set up your portfolio."

"I'd really prefer that you send it over," he said looking at her. "I'd rather deal directly with you."

"Sure," she agreed. The two shook hands, and London watched as he stepped into the elevator. Turning on her heels and heading back to her office, she had to call the girls. London had to make sure that everyone was still on tonight, including Sade.

# *Chapter Eight*

Raven pulled into the driveway and let out a sigh. Turning off the ignition she sat back in her seat looked towards the car next to her shaking her head. It had been a while since she'd been over, and if Raven had it her way she wouldn't be here now.

Sade had been one of her best friends throughout college and had been one of the people that she trusted the most, but due to the recent events in all of the girl's lives. Sade was now on the outs with the girls, and Raven didn't see the need to continue the charade of keeping her close.

The last time that Raven had been at Sade's house, she didn't feel comfortable in the woman's home. Sade seemed to ask questions about everything pertaining to London, from her finances to her parents. Although Raven had always played down what London or her family was involved in, it still didn't stop Sade from asking questions.

Stepping out of the car Raven remembered the last time that she had come over to Sade's house. The night had started out like any other, and then turned into twenty-one questions with London being the topic of discussion. When Raven had left Sade's house, she immediately told the group what she'd suspected. No one in the group could've been for certain whether or not

Sade was really an informant and had taped the conversations she'd had with the girls, but that didn't stop Black from hiring someone to investigate Sade.

Unlike Sade and London, Raven hadn't been raised in the lap of luxury. She'd hailed from the streets of South Side Chicago and knew the street politics better than anyone when it came to associating with snakes.

Walking towards Sade's door she began to feel sick. The door swung open before she could knock, and there she was in all her glory, Sade. Standing with one hand on the doorknob and the other cradling a glass of white wine, she smiled as Raven walked through the door.

"I was starting to think you weren't going to show up," Sade said giving her a hug.

Raven returned the hug and looked around the living room at Karma and London who were seated on the cream-colored sofa sipping wine, with a spread of fresh fruit, cheese, and crackers on the coffee table in front of them. She gave both them a look and shook her head. London and Karma looked at one another and then back towards Raven before bursting into laughter.

"What's so funny?" Sade asked closing the door. She walked into the living room and sat on the sofa across from the two women and patted the seat next to her for Raven.

"Nothing," Karma said waving her off. "You wouldn't understand."

Sade looked at the women and smiled sweetly. "Now that we're all able to get together," she said grabbing the glass off the table and pouring a glass from Raven. "What's been up with everyone? I feel like I've missed so much."

"Same shit different day," Karma said folding her legs in front of her.

"London what's been going on with you," Sade asked looking at her. "How're your parents.?"

Karma and Raven both took a sip from their cups as they looked at London and Sade. London hadn't mentioned her parents since Christmas, and no one had brought their names up.

London hadn't had the chance to grieve, and from the way she reacted at the double funeral they couldn't tell if she held some form of regret for the role she played that resulted in both of their deaths. Although London considered her father a trader to the family, he was still her father at the end of everything. She couldn't say that she missed him more than her mother, but she did wish at times that they both were around.

London nodded her head lightly and smiled. "Everything is great," she answered. "My parents are fine as well."

Both Karma and Raven let out a sigh of relief as London sat back in her seat. For the remainder of the evening it was like old times, where the women would sip cocktails and discuss the latest that was going on in their lives. Each woman there with an ulterior motive, and each with their own agenda. As London and Sade looked at one another neither knew that either would ultimately be the demise of the other.

---

Vine stepped out of his car and made hurried steps towards the house. Noticing Face's car parked out front he shook his head knowing that twiddle dee and twiddle dumb were on some stupid shit. Vine had always been down for the come-up and had done his fair share of stupid shit all in the name of gangbanging, but now that the stakes were higher and he was moving in circles he'd never imagined, he no longer had time for the stupid shit that Black and Face seemed to do just for kicks.

He shook his head as he opened the door and looked around the disheveled state of the living room. A woman sat tied to a chair by a child's jump-rope, and a man lay on the floor bleeding from every orifice of his body. Looking over at the two men who were wiping their hands with towels they'd found in a cabinet, he looked at both of them and scuffed.

"What the fuck happened here?" he said walking through the room.

"You remember Bo," Black said looking down at the man who lay unconscious.

Vine shook his head and walked over towards him. "Yeah I remember this nigga. Don't he owe like sixteen grand?"

"Yep," Face said stalking over to where he stood. "And neither he, nor his bitch can tell us what happened to the money."

Vine turned and looked at the woman. "Damn," he said looking her over. "What the fuck was you doing fucking with this herb ass nigga."

"That's a lot of pussy that's about to go to waste," Face said reaching into his pocket and removing a cigarette.

"I didn't even think about that shit," Vine said looking at the woman and shaking his head. "Anybody else in the house?"

"Naw," Black said tossing the towel on the man. "It's empty. Her kids at her moms house."

"Cool," Vine said looking. "So what you want to do my nigga? You didn't get the money, and you got a nigga on the floor who may or may not be alive, and a fucking witness."

The woman's eyes doubled in size as she listened to the men talking. She knew what was coming next, she was going to die all because she had made the choice of picking the wrong nigga to date. She started screaming but the sounds were muffled thanks to the gag that was in her mouth.

"What's that baby?" Face said in a taunting tone. "You wanna talk."

He walked over towards the woman and slapped her across the face. The blow was so hard that he knocked the woman over. "You should've told us where the money was at before we even had to do all this," he snapped and turning back towards the men. "What we doing?"

"Exactly," Vine said looking at Black.

"Fuck it. Kill both these mothafucka's and burn this bitch down," he said as he stepped over the man. "Face make sure you pick up them towels and them cigarette butts. No DNA."

Both Vine and Face shook their head in agreement, producing the guns that were tucked in their waistbands into the picture.

Boom. Boom. Boom. Boom. Boom. Boom. Boom.

They fired their guns into both bodies until their clips were empty. Face went about the task of grabbing the towels they'd used to wipe their hands, and grabbing the cigarette butts that he'd dropped on the carpet, going around the house wiping off the surfaces that they'd touched while in the house.

Vine had gone out to his car, and returned with a can of gasoline, pouring the gas in every room in the house, he walked into the kitchen and turned on the stove so that the gas filled the room. As he and Face made their way towards the front of the house, Vine reached into his pocket and removed a book of matches. Lighting one match before lighting the rest and throwing them into the house. He walked out as the flames engulfed the entire living room.

All of the men hopped into the cars and drove off the street as the house burst into flames and the sound of an explosion filled the air.

# Chapter Nine

The sound of the phone ringing caused her to stir. Reaching over and grabbing his cell off the nightstand London looked at the name sprawled across and frowned.

"What?" she said into the phone. Her tone was low, husky informing the person on the other end that she was sleep and that they'd just woke her up.

"London," Vine's voice screamed into the phone. "Where's Black?"

London opened her eyes and looked around the dark room, trying to adjust her eyes. She knew that he was in the house because his cell was on the nightstand, but when she didn't see any reminisce of the man in the room she sat up in the bed.

"I don't know," she said honestly. "He's here, but he's not right here."

"I know this is a lot especially at three in the morning," Vine said in an even tone. "But I need you to give that nigga the phone."

"What's wrong?" she asked.

Vine let out a sigh, "Three of the spots just got raided."

London frowned as she stood from the bed. "What do you mean the spots got raided?"

Opening the door she looked down the hallway, and shook her head before walking towards the stairs.

"Just what I said," he answered.

"Black," London yelled as she walked down the stairs.

'This nigga,' she thought as she noticed him asleep on the couch. London walked over towards Black and gently nudge his arm. He opened his eyes slightly and pulled her on top of him.

"Why're you on the couch?" she asked looking at him.

"I ate and was down here watching the game, and a nigga fell asleep," he said kissing her neck and running his hands over her ass.

"Vine's on the phone," she said placing the phone to his ear.

"Yeah cuz," he said in a tone that expressed his annoyance. Black was quiet for a while as he listened to Vine talk. "Aight let me know what happens. I'll have London call Raven once them niggas is booked."

London climbed off of him and moved towards the other end of the couch.

"I'll call Raven once we know what's what," he said ending the call. He looked over at London and grabbed her hand pulling her back towards him.

"It's three in the morning and I have to work in the morning," she said as she tried to climb off of him. With every movement that London moved, Black seemed to pull her back in the position he needed her in. Sliding his hands up the sleepshirt that she was wearing realizing that she wasn't wearing any panties a smile came to his face.

"I need to be sleep," she said as she reached under her. Placing her hands in the basketball shorts that he was wearing she began to slowly tug at his manhood.

"Raise up a minute," he said as he lifted her hips. London did as she was told and watched as he slid his shorts down bringing his erect penis to the party. London smirked as she slid off of him and landed on her knees. Black sat up on the couch and adjusted himself into a sitting position.

London grabbed ahold of his manhood and slowly took him into her mouth. She moved her head up and down the full length of his shaft, making sure that her hands moved up and down him as she sucked his dick. Taking in him to the back of her throat, and seemingly making his dick disappear down her throat as she did. London worked his dick until she felt his dick jump while in her mouth. Feeling himself about to explode he grabbed the back of her head, as he shot his child support bills down her throat.

Wiping the side of her mouth London stood to her feet and looked at him. Black looked down at his partially erect penis and stood to his feet. Gently tossing London onto the couch, so that her back was to him, he reached down opening her legs, placing his dick at the entrance of her honey box he penetrated her.

No sooner than London could let out a moan, Black's phone rang. Reaching down and picking the phone up off the table he looked at the name that was sprawled across the screen and grimaced.

"Baby don't answer," she said in a breathy tone. London began throwing her ass back onto his dick.

"I got to," he said as he continued to pound into her.

London let out a moan, as Black answered the phone.

"Nigga," the voice boomed through the phone. "Get to the hood right now. Some shits going down."

"If it's about the raid then nigga I already know," he said never losing his rhythm.

"Fuck the raid," the man spoke into the phone. "Some niggas from the Senate just came through and shot JoJo."

Black stopped stroking London and was silent for a moment. "Give me twenty and I'm on the way," he said ending the call.

London looked back at him and frowned. "What's wrong now?" she asked with an attitude.

"The fucking Senate."

---

London watched as Black headed up the stairs. She'd heard what he said, and she knew that they were the truth, but what she didn't know was how.

The Senate began and ended with the Originals, once they were killed it seemed as though the Senate had disappeared never to be heard from again. Now that

Black had stated that the Senate was back, and had just killed one of his friends, she knew that it was only a matter of time before blood was spilt on the streets of LA.

Standing from the couch London headed after him, walking into the bedroom, she noticed him standing in the closet. She wouldn't have paid it any mind normally, but what she saw caused her to question exactly who the man she lay next to every night was.

An entire row of clothes had been moved, and behind them sat a faux wall that once the cover was removed displayed several guns. London sat down on the bed as she watched Black remove two nine-millimeter handguns, and a semi-automatic, replacing the drywall that covered the space, and the rack of clothes.

"What the fuck are you doing?" she asked.

Black turned and looked at her, and the scowl that was written across his face let her know that questions at this point were pointless. Black didn't say a word as he loaded the guns into a duffel bag.

He walked over towards London kissed her on the forehead and disappeared out the door. London didn't know what to make of what she had saw, and what had just happened. Grabbing her phone off the nightstand, she dialed Karma's number.

"I'm on my way to you right now," she said answering on the first ring.

"Ok," London said just above a whisper.

"I'll be there in a minute. Raven should get there before me. Let her in."

"I thought they were gone."

"We all did. London," Karma said into the phone. "Now is not the time to fold. Pull yourself together and once we all get there, we'll talk about what to do next."

London shook her head as if Karma could see her and ended the call.

# *Chapter Ten*

Closing the file that was in front of her Raven sat her hands on the table and intertwined her fingers. Looking at the three people that sat opposite her with smug looks on their faces and she wished she could wipe them off, permanently.

"You all know as well as I do," she started. "LAPD is capable of just about anything. Now look, if you'd like to sit around for months on end, going through a bunch of half heard, half doctored phone conversations and see how well you do, then be my guests."

"It's not just talks on the wire," the man spoke looking at her. "We've got seized money and a lot of dope on a table from several cook houses."

"And a lot of violence," the woman spoke. She looked around the room and frowned. Looking across the table at the young attorney, she couldn't help but to smirk. Knowing that this was the first major case that the woman had taken, and from the looks of things the woman was in way over her head. She knew that once they got her in court she'd be able to eat her up, at least that's what she was hoping for.

They had her clients on drug trafficking, drug possession, and murder. It was an open and shut case if she had to say so herself.

"All of which stops short of Mr. Peters," Raven said looking at the three individuals sitting across from her. "You know this."

The three people sitting across from her looked at her and shook their heads. It seemed as though they had all underestimated the young attorney.

"All of which except for the Compton busts," the officer said in annoyance looking at her. "That one he eats."

Raven looked around the room and smirked.

Legal books filled the wall to her left held in an oak wood bookshelf the walls had been painted an olive color with brown oak paneling. Sitting across the oak table staring at her sat the DDA's Brandon Tyler, Leslie Chambers, and officer Cornell.

Raven had been hired by the family to take care of what they considered a small problem, it wasn't until Raven had reviewed the case file that she'd learned that there were wiretaps connecting her client Michael Peters to the Royal's. Hours of tapes discussing drug transports, photos of the drugs and cash from various stash houses around the city waited in the boxes in her office.

Although she hadn't gone through all of the boxes, she knew that her client was guilty, hell they all were, but that wasn't her job to condemn him. Raven was being paid to get him off, and if she couldn't do that, she was at least to get a sentence reduction.

"Maybe he does. Maybe he pleads to one count of attempted possession and takes what maybe three, four. Maybe he can arrange for everyone you have on those tapes to follow suit. Maybe you get five-year pleas from those with no prior felony convictions, ten years for those with one prior, fifteen for two or more."

"What about the murders? Is your client willing to testify that the Royals are behind the murders?" Brandon asked looking at her.

"Maybe we acknowledge you've got Mr. Peters cold for the wounding of a police officer during the raid," Raven said.

The three individuals on the other side of the table looked at one another shaking their heads.

"That's not enough," Leslie said looking at her.

"Naming co-conspirators? For that kind of cooperation, I'm willing to offer Mr. Peters 5 years," Brandon said looking at Raven.

"No," Raven said looking at them. "Mr. Peters has no ties to this 'Royal's' as you claim."

"We have information stating that not only does Mr. Peters have ties to the Royal's, but he's one of their top lieutenants."

Raven chuckled, "Like I've stated. We're not implicating my client in any crimes that he hasn't committed."

Leslie sighed. "Assets? What about the properties?"

"You take whatever trucks and cars you can link to the drug trafficking, and, of course whatever cash you've seized."

"There's dozens of properties," Officer Cornel said reaching into the folder in front of him. "A funeral parlor, strip club, warehouses."

"Are those properties in my clients name?" Raven asked looking at him.

"They're linked to the Royal's organization," Cornel said looking at her.

Raven shook her head. "I'm sorry officer, being that those properties aren't directly linked to my client then there's no need to discuss them. You get the cars because you can link them to illegal activity, but there's nothing left in Mr. Peter's name to take."

Brandon looked around the room, perturbed. For the past six years he'd been going after the Royal's, and after failed attempt after failed attempt. He knew he had them dead to rights, but what he wasn't expecting was the woman sitting across from him.

The criminal attorney that had been hired to meet him in court wasn't playing fair. He'd expected the people caught in the raid to be represented by an overworked underpaid public defender, but when the woman walked in dressed in a fifteen hundred dollar navy business suit, and five inch heels, her makeup perfectly done and just enough to not transform her look but to enhance the beauty that was already there, he knew that he was in for a challenge.

Raven was representing four of the six people arrested two nights before and had managed to get three of her clients released on bail. Brandon didn't know who the woman was, but he had to give credit where it was due. She was a damn good attorney, who'd managed to get every shred of evidence sent to her office within 24-hours and had seemingly went over everything in preparation for the meeting.

"So," Brandon said looking at her. "You keep most of the money, most of the real estate and the Royal's stay on the street."

"If you can provide proof that these so-called Royal's exist, I suggest you file a charge against them," Raven said in a matter of fact tone. "Otherwise it's my understanding that nothing in all those hours of tapes implicates my client for anything other than what he's being charged with."

Brandon sat back in his chair letting out an exasperated sigh. "Three or four years aint enough," he said shaking his head. "Not for a member of the criminal organiztion."

"No?" Raven said with a smirk on her face looking at them. "Make an offer."

They all looked at Raven with a scowl on their faces. She didn't know what was to come next, but she knew that it was going to be big, and it would be a defining moment in her career and with the family.

---

Sitting in the back of the crowded court room holding a newspaper. The pages had been turned to the Business section, and he'd barely taken a glance down at the paper in his hands.

Dressed in a tailored Armani suit that clung to his frame, his smooth light brown complexion looked as though it had been kissed by the sun, gold wired frames covered his big brown eyes. Running his hand over his neatly trimmed beard as Vine watched as everyone stood to their feet as the door behind the judge's seat opened.

"Case number 6980-16 in the circuit court of Los Angeles City now in session, please be seated," the bailiff said as he stood next to the podium.

Vine took a seat and looked around the room. The box that held many of the members of his organization was to the brim as the men waited for their cases to be heard by the judge, learning their fates by the end of the day. The room had been filled with men and women alike as they waited to see the outcomes of their loved one's cases.

"First up," the judge said becoming comfortable in his seat.

Vine watched from the back of the room as the young, black attorney on the right side of the room stood to his feet, standing behind the desk. Looking down at the papers on the desk, he cleared his throat, and adjusted his clothes.

"State versus Michael Peters, your honor," the man spoke in a clear sharp tone. "One count of possession with intent to distribute, to it, a kilo of heroin."

"You have with it a statement of facts?" the judge asked.

"Yes your honor," he said. "Mr. Peters is offering a plea of guilty in exchange for a maximum of seven years in CDC. In consideration of the following agreed-upon facts. On or about the date of January 17, 2016 in the jurisdiction of Scottsdale, Arizona officer Franklin Barracks of Scottsdale police department effected a traffic stop on a rented Nissan Altima traveling westbound near exit 93. That traffic stop resulted from information learned from electronic surveillance of Mr. Peters, by detectives assigned to a special detail under the command of a city narcotics supervisor. A search of the vehicle which was rented from the Enterprise location at LAX airport, revealed that a kilogram of nearly pure heroin was concealed beneath the spare tire in the trunk. In accepting this plea, Mr. Peters acknowledges his role in procuring with the intent to dilute, package, and sell retail amounts of heroin."

Vine stood from his seat, as the district attorney continued his argument and looked around the room. Raven turned around catching his eyes before turning back towards the judge.

Adjusting his suit jacket he walked out of the court room. Reaching into his pocket removing his cellphone, he headed for the exit.

Three men dressed in street clothes passed him, and as he locked eyes with the men he chuckled. They were cops that he'd seen around the neighborhood, whom the hood niggas affectionally called Pop-Outs, because they would pop out of their cars for just about any infraction.

Stepping onto the stairs of Los Angeles Superior courthouse, he took in a deep pull of the fresh air. Vine had seen the inside of the courthouse more times than he could count, and he was just glad that he now had the option of leaving whenever he wanted, and not when they told him he could.

Scrolling through the contacts on his phone as he descended the stairs. Listening to the line trill in his ear as he walked towards the parking garage that he'd left his car.

"What's up?" Black's voice boomed through the phone. "We good?"

"Yea we good. She got him seven," Vine said giving him the blow by blow of what he'd heard before leaving out of the courtroom.

"Aight."

"Meet me on the 8," Vine said walking into the chain link fenced parking structure. "I got some shit to say and I can't say it over the phone."

"I'm at Jacks. So call me when you get over there."

"Say less," Vine said. "I'm on my way."

He ended the call and walked over towards his car. Pulling out the parking garage into the heavy downtown traffic. Turning his radio up to the highest level it would go, he glanced into his rearview mirror.

A wicked grin crossed his face as he noticed the car sitting behind him. LAPD had gone through the tax payers money investing in a ton of unmarked cars, and as he switched lanes so the car could catch up to him, or pass him his suspicions were confirmed when the plates on the car didn't hold the normal tags but instead read, California Exempt.

The car passed him, and as the officers in the car looked over at Vine as they passed, he shook his head and scowled in disgust.

'It's about to be a hot ass summer,' he thought as he nodded his head to the sounds of DJ Khaled's latest album.

# *Chapter Eleven*

Vine pulled his car onto 38<sup>th</sup> place off of Western Avenue, pulling his car into the available park on the corner. Turning down the radio he grabbed his cellphone and sent a text to Black letting him know that he had made it on the block before climbing out of his car and heading towards the house across the street.

The summer rays had everyone that lived on the block out onto the streets. Women wore next to nothing not leaving much to the imagination, kids ran up and down the streets playing in and out of traffic on skateboards, scooters, and bikes. Looking around the block he nodded towards a couple of people he had known from around the way, before walking into the yard of his boy's mother's house.

Slapping hands with a couple of the men that were congregating in the yard, before climbing the three stairs and taking a seat on the bannister.

"What up my nigga?" TG said giving him a pound. "A nigga aint seen you in a minute. What's been up?"

"Shit," Vine said reaching into his pocket and removing a pack of camels and a lighter. Lighting the cigarette he looked at him and smirked. "You know how shit go. Same shit different toilet."

"I hear that shit," he said taking a pull from the blunt in his hand. "So, what brings you to the land."

"I needed to talk to y'all niggas," he said looking around the yard. "I'm just waiting on Black to get here."

TG shook his head as both he and Vine looked towards the front door. They watched as a young nigga named Style walked onto the front porch. Neither man could understand how the boy had received his name, because personal style was something that he didn't have.

He wasn't much to look at, he was tall, skinny, with dark skin that was ashy and in desperate need of Vaseline. Nothing really stood out about the young man to any of the people around the way, other than the fact that he was a runner for the Royal's. He didn't know much, but he did know enough to be able to handle a couple of transports, which resulted in him getting a little change. Enough change to have the little birds around the way clocking for him.

"Nah, it's a shipment coming in tonight," Style said. "After I do the drop I can-"

Vine stood to his feet and grabbed the phone out of the boy's hand. Throwing the phone to the ground he began to step on it, smashing it to bits.

Style looked at Vine as if he had lost his mind, and before he could protest. Vine had grabbed the boy around the neck, choking him. The amount of force that he had on his neck caused him to pick the boy up a few inches off the ground.

Everyone in the yard turned and watched as Vine stood there choking the boy without so much as saying a word. After seeing enough, and noticing Black's jaguar pulling onto the block, TG walked over to Face and placed his hand on his shoulder.

"Let the nigga live, cuz," he said. Vine turned to look at him. The scowl that was written across his face was enough to make a weaker nigga scared, but TG wasn't the average nigga. Vine let go of the boy's throat and looked from Style to TG and then towards the car that was coming to a stop in the middle of the street.

"They got wires," he said loud enough for everyone in the yard to hear. "Every mothafuckin phone is tapped."

"Who?" TG asked. "The boys."

Vine shook his head. "Yea. I just left Lil' Mike's arraignment. The mothafucka's got a wiretap. They got tapes of conversations, and niggas like this," he said turning towards Style. "Is running they fucking mouths on the phone, about to get all of us sent upstate."

"I…. I wouldn't do shit to get us crossed up," Style said while rubbing his neck.

"Nigga I don't know that," TG said looking at him. "For all I know the mothafucka you were on the phone telling our business to was the cops."

"From now on nobody talks business over the phone," Vine said looking around the yard. "You got a shipment you talk to the mothafucka from a pay phone, you do a pickup you talk in mothafuckin person."

"The raid the other night could've been avoided," Black said stepping into the yard. "Y'all leaving to much shit in one spot."

"Exactly," Vine agreed. "From now on you niggas need three, four spots a piece. Put them shits in these knocks names and keep that shit moving."

He walked as the men in the yard shook their heads in agreement before turning towards Black. "Walk with me nigga," he said tapping him on the arm. The two men began heading out of the yard, and Vine stopped and looked back at Style.

"Take that nigga on a ride," he said to the man closest to the gate before walking off. The people in the yard watched as the two men walked away.

Everyone in the yard could feel the heat rising and it wasn't from the sun. Hell it didn't matter whether it came in the form of the summer heat, or the heat from the police, none of them knew or cared. But what they did know for certain was that it was going to be one hell of a summer. Especially if things didn't change soon.

---

"How's London?" Vine asked as he and Black walked down the street.

"She going through it. She thought the Senate was done for, especially after she had gotten rid of Stone. To hear that they've sprung back up and are taken aim at niggas on the streets," Black said shaking his head. "She's feeling some type of way."

Vine shook his head. "Understandable. Who would've thought that these punk ass mothafucka's were still being fed?"

"She wants to know who's behind it," Black said looking at him.

"She got too many irons in the fire right now. She trying to run the family, run a business, find out who's behind that damn site."

"Thankfully aint no post been out about this shit," Black said.

"It would've done our asses some good to have a heads up that these mothafucka's was back on the scene."

Black shook his head in agreement. "What's this shit you were saying about a wire?"

Vine shook his head and looked at his boy. "Apparently they have a wiretap in place. I didn't see any Feds in court so the shit must be local for now," he said in a matter of fact tone. "Speaking of which. Maya got back to me on that shit about ol' girl."

"Who?"

"Sade," Vine said as a devilish grin spread across his face.

Black took a step back and looked at him. "She working?"

"Yep," Vine answered. "Has been since she met London in college. So far, she hasn't been able to get anything on her, but once the feds get wind of this shit. You know how shit's going to play out."

Black nodded his head in agreement. "We need to meet at the house tonight. Call Face and tell that nigga to be there by nine."

"Say less."

# *Chapter Twelve*

Sitting across from the three women in the crowded restaurant in Marina del Rey, London casually took sips from the whiskey sour before her, as she listened to the women tell her of their struggles.

Their loved ones were facing five to twenty years in prison leaving them with no viable income, and no way to make up for the loss of income that was inevitably coming their way, she couldn't help but to look down at her watch. It wasn't that she was tired of listening to the women talk about everything they were losing, but she was becoming impatient as she had to wait for Black to arrive before she could deliver her decision as to what to do for the women.

Raven had called her after the meeting with the deputy district attorneys and given her a heads up that members of the Royals were looking at football numbers, and no matter how much evidence she had gotten thrown out of court, the wiretap that was in place, was the prosecutions main defense and sealed many of their fates. Giving the State enough to toss more than a few years at the men she'd represented that day.

"I don't know what I'm supposed to do," the woman named Kayla said as she looked around the table. "Blue took care of everything, and now that he's not here I don't know what I'm supposed to do."

"Don't worry about it," London said taking a sip from her drink. "We'll take care of things."

"How? I mean I don't mean to question you and all, but I need to know exactly how? And for how long will this last," the other woman Olivia asked.

London looked at all three of the women and placed a smile on her lips. Kayla was pretty, London had to give her that. Her dark brown complexion was smooth, slanted eyes, and perfectly arched brows, standing four feet eleven, with a small waist, round ass, and average breast size, London knew that there wasn't a man on the streets that would have risked it all to snatch her up.

Olivia was yellow, many would consider her a red bone. She was tall, thick, and stacked. Her thirty-inch weave was neatly done, long acrylic nails, and false lashes. It wasn't hard for London to see where majority of her man's money went. Olivia's perky 38 D's were freshly done, her waist was snatched as if she were wearing a waist trainer when she wasn't, and her ass was so fat that it made London stop and stare.

Destiny was the only woman at the table who hadn't spoken during the thirty minutes that they were seated at the table, other than the simple pleasantries the woman didn't say much. London could tell that she was young, probably no older than nineteen. Her firm breasts, and round ass sat at its regular proportions. She was light skinned and looked as though she were mixed with black and Asian, giving her baby doll features.

Unlike the other women who were dressed as if they were going to the club, instead of a meeting with the woman who ultimately held their financial future in her hands, Destiny was dressed simple, jeans and a shirt. No jewels, no fake nails, hair, or eyelashes.

Looking up from the plate setting before her she looked over at London locking eyes with her.

"What is it that you want?" London asked looking at her.

Destiny shrugged. "I don't know," she said looking from her to the women sitting next to her. "I just know that I'm not used to having someone take care of me other than Mike."

London shook her head. "I understand that. But, what do you want?"

Olivia scuffed. "I know what I want."

"I didn't ask you," London snapped looking at her. She turned her attention back to the girl, whose eyes diverted back towards the plates in front of her.

London sighed as she took a sip from the drink on the table. She turned her head slightly as she watched him walk towards the table.

He'd gone for a shave to edge up his beard, and a haircut. Dressed in a white polo shirt, and black jeans with a pair of black and white Jordan's on his feet. London noticed the three gold chains on his neck, gold watch, and diamond stud in his ear the closer he got. Standing to her feet, as he walked over towards her. London hugged Black and moved towards the seat to his right, sitting across from the women.

"Black," she said looking at him and then towards the women. "This is Olivia, Kayla, and Destiny."

Black nodded towards the women and turned his attention towards London. London looked at him and smiled as she noticed the waitress coming towards their table. Each one placed their order, and Black waited for the woman to walk away before speaking.

"Why am I here?" he asked looking at London.

"These are the women that were with the guys that were busted in the raid. Being that they're doing a bid for us I thought that we'd offer them some kind of compensation to tie them over until the men are free."

Black looked at London and chuckled, "I already took care of the families."

"What family?" Olivia said with an attitude. "Because I damn sure didn't get shit."

Black looked at her with a scowl on his face. "That's because his wife got everything."

London looked from Olivia to Black, "What?"

"She didn't tell you?" he said grabbing London's drink. "Yea that nigga Slim Goody got a wife. I sent my people to talk to her this morning once the deal was made."

"So why the fuck didn't nobody tell me?" Olivia asked her neck snaking as she looked at him.

Black laughed and then looked at London. "Talk to her before her ass don't make it home tonight," he said with a slight chuckle.

London looked from him to Olivia, and then towards the other women. "Is there something that any of you would like to tell me? Is Blue married? What about Lil' Mike?"

Kayla and Destiny both shook their heads no. "Ok," London said looking at Olivia. "Here's what I can offer you. Being that you weren't married to the man, and you two were only fucking. Ten thousand should be enough to tie you over until the next meal ticket comes along."

"Ten grand?" Olivia said confused. Olivia was a hood chick to the core, and even though she had never seen ten grand in one place at one time, she couldn't help but to feel insulted. After all of the shit that she had been through with Slim over the past two years, she felt as though she needed ten thousand dollars for each year she dealt with his psychotic ass.

"If that's what she's offering. I suggest you take that and run with it," Black said looking at her.

"That's not even fair," Olivia said getting louder. London looked around the restaurant as people began staring in their direction, causing her to become uncomfortable.

"I'm going to need you to lower your voice," London said in an even tone.

"Naw, fuck that. Y'all trying to low ball me. Meanwhile my man is doing a bid for y'all," Olivia snapped.

London shook her head and looked towards Black. Black looked at the men at the table down from them and nodded his head, giving them a signal. The men stood to their feet and began walking in their direction.

"Y'all owe me," Olivia continued. "You think I won't burn y'all shit to the ground you got another thing coming."

London sat back in her seat as the men approached the table. They stepped over to where Black was sitting and she watched as he leaned over, whispered something to the men and headed for Olivia.

"Go with them," Black said in a less than pleasant tone.

"Hell no," she said folding her arms across her chest.

"I got enough money to pay everybody in this restaurant to say that they aint never seen yo face before, and enough money to have yo ass killed right where you sit. So, I'm gon tell you again. Go with them."

London and the ladies watched as Olivia stood to her feet, grabbed her purse and was escorted out of the restaurant.

"Now anybody else wanna start some shit," he asked looking at the three women remaining.

Destiny and Kayla both shook their heads no. London turned to Black and shook her head. He winked and gave her a slight smile, as the waitress appeared with their order.

The rest of the meal they covered the basics. London had offered both women a substantial amount of money to say that they never saw Olivia that day and offered to cover their expenses for the next two years under the condition they both found a way to make money to provide for themselves.

London had gotten both of the women's phone numbers, she knew that if push came to shove Karma would hire one of them, and if not, she was sure to find something for them.

London reached into her bag pulling her credit card from her wallet so that she could take care of the meal, she looked over at Black who was ogling her as if she were the main course at his favorite restaurant.

"What?" she asked looking at him.

"Nothing," he said looking at her. "What you about to get into after this?"

London shrugged. "Home. I invited the girls over for drinks and movie."

"You wanna talk about this shit with the Senate," he said.

"I don't know," she answered honestly.

"We either talk about it so that you can have a say in the matter, or you let us handle it."

"Then handle it," she said looking at him.

"Take a walk with me," he said standing from the table and heading for the door.

London waited for the waiter to come to the table to retrieve the bill. Once she had gotten her card back, she headed for the exit. Black was standing next to the door smoking a cigarette. London waved her hand in front of her face, and then looked at him.

"Where to?" she asked looking at him.

Walking along the boardwalk Black absently grabbed London's hand, interlocking his fingers in hers. The heat had finally subsided, and the breeze coming from the marina carried in a wave of cool air, as the two talked. It had been a while since the two had been able to go out alone, and even though there was a lot that was going on within the family none of it mattered at this moment.

"How's the business?" he asked.

London shrugged. "It's good. It's a lot, and sometimes I feel like I can't handle it, but it's going really well. How's the business?"

He chuckled. "Other than this shit with the wiretap, and the raids. Not bad."

"I guess we can count out the party you wanted to throw a few months ago," she said looking at him.

"Nah," he said shaking his head. "We got enough going on right now, and what the fuck would be celebrating anyway, our crews getting locked up left and right."

"I wonder who they flipped."

"It's not a wonder of who they flipped," he said in a matter of fact tone. "From what I'm hearing the Royals are ringing all kinds of bells downtown, and the shit is making me uncomfortable if I'm being honest."

"I know," London agreed. "This is a lot. This is why I didn't want to be a part of this shit in the first place. When you kill one problem, you end up with three others. Springing seemingly out of nowhere."

"It comes with the life."

"This isn't the life that I wanted," she said looking at him. London pulled her hand from his as she stopped walking. "Black what if I told you that I wanted more than this."

"More than what?"

"This," she said motioning around her. "Yea it's good, don't get me wrong. But, there's a whole fucking world out there and here we are. Selling drugs, blackmailing government officials, doing shit that we don't have no business doing."

Black shook his head knowing where she was headed. "You want out?"

London shook her head. "No," she said looking at him. "I just want to be able to do what I want to do."

"Is that what you plan on talking to the girls about tonight? You plan on telling this shit to Vine and Face."

London sighed and continued walking. "No," she said. "I want to know why you never told me that you had someone on Sade. I also want to know what you came back with."

Black chuckled. "Who told you?"

"Pillow talk trumps everything else," she said nudging him.

"She's working with the feds. Apparently, she's known about you and who your parents were for a long time. The crimes her parents were charged with are white collar, and of course the sentences they received could be reduced or overturned for the right information."

London sighed and grabbed ahold of the railing as she felt her knees go weak.

"What'd you have in mind?"

Black looked at her and chuckled. "It's on y'all, but I do have something in mind if y'all don't handle it."

# _Chapter Thirteen_

Black stared out of the window watching as the kids played in the park. The innocence of the children who played on slides, swings, or playing tag always amazed him. He had done so much fucked up shit in his life that he couldn't remember a time that he didn't have the weight of the world on his shoulders. As he sat in the parking lot leaning against the hood of his car smoking a blunt, half listening to the man standing next to him as he spoke.

The connections that came from the Originals touched a lot of high-profile names, but nothing compared to the connections he'd made on his own. His cousin Raymond was an officer with LAPD had called him earlier that day asking him to meet with him to discuss the latest details of the cases of the men in his crew as well as what he'd learned about Black.

Black had tuned him out several times throughout their conversation, only listening to the parts that were pertinent to himself. Taking a deep pull from the blunt, he blew out the smoke and looked at the man.

"When are they passing down the indictments?" he asked.

"No later than Monday," he answered. "I suggest you get everything together, because it looks like they're trying to throw the book at you."

Black frowned and looked at him. For the past six months Black had known that it would only be a matter of time before he'd be sitting in a jail cell. He'd known from the first raid back in January that they were coming his way, and that they probably didn't have enough information to pursue an indictment at the time. After everything he'd done on the streets in his life, and getting away with everything scot free Black was now half stepping.

"What about girly?" Black asked taking in a deep pull of the blunt.

"No word on her. They don't know anything about her, yet," he answered.

Black shook his head. "Ok. Let me run this shit past my crew and then I'll get back to you."

"Sounds like a plan," he said giving him a pound and stepping out of the car.

"Aye," Black said calling after him. "Make sure that you tell Aunt Cassie I said hi, and that I'll make it to Sunday dinner."

"Might as well," he chuckled. "Could be the last Sunday dinner yo ass have in a long time."

Black flipped him off as he climbed into his car and starting his ignition. Pulling out of the parking lot, he decided to head for London. Being that it was the middle of the workday he knew that he could find her at her office. Weaving in and out of LA's heavy afternoon traffic, heading towards London's office, the only thought that came to mind was how was he going to explain this shit to her.

---

"This is London," she said into the receiver. Glancing down at the computer monitor, before pressing in a series of numbers.

"Hello Ms. Clark, this is Brandon," the voice boomed through the other end.

London smiled, sitting back in her chair. "Hello Mr. Tyler. What can I do for you today?"

"I wanted to know if you'd be able to schedule a meeting for later this afternoon," he spoke. "I have a few revisions for my portfolio that I'd like to discuss with you."

"Not a problem," she replied. "Was there something wrong with the initial portfolio?"

He chuckled, "No there weren't any problems. I just wanted to add a secondary name to the accounts. As well as a new investment option."

London shook her head. "Ok," she said looking at the desk top calendar that sat to her left. "I have a three fifteen and a four thirty available."

"I'll see you at three fifteen."

"Not a problem. I'll have my assistant let me know when you arrive."

"I'll see you later this afternoon," he replied ending the call.

London placed the phone back on the receiver and looked down at her computer monitor as a smile came to her face. There was something about being in the man's presence that was a welcomed feeling.

He'd been her client for over two months and had tried to no avail to convince her to go out with him. Even with everything going on around her, and the need to do something new, Brandon still couldn't convince the woman to go out with him.

London was in a good place in her relationship with Black and didn't see the need to step out on him. Although whenever her and Brandon were together it was refreshing to talk about something other than street politics, and even though she found his life interesting she wouldn't cross the line.

He'd talk about his work for hours on end going past their scheduled meeting times. London had discovered so much about the man whom she only intended to conduct business with, that it made her that much more intrigued. There was no mistaking the attraction between the two, but London wasn't that kind of chick. When she loved a man it was him and only him that she wanted to be with.

"Ms. Clark," Thomas's voice boomed through the intercom. "Mr. Harrison is here to see you."

"Send him back," London said as she closed the file on the computer.

Standing from her desk London walked over towards the window. Running her hand over the Alexander McQueen knee length dress that she was wearing, as she stood looking out of the window. Her spiral curls danced down her back cascading over the back of the dress, four-inch patent leather black heels with gold chains that wrapped around the ankles, a three-row diamond necklace around her neck, and five carat diamond hoop earrings in her ear.

The door opening made a creaking sound as Black walked into the room. London could smell the distinct traces of weed as the door closed, turning to look at the man of the hour. She hadn't seen him since the night before. Black had been in the streets trying to track down members of the Senate.

The night before Black had delivered the information that he'd received on Sade to the Board. Vine and Face had already heard the news earlier that day, so it was the girls who were left to decide what move came next. Black didn't waste any time letting them know that they had a month to handle Sade or he was going to send a team of killers for her. There was nothing London could do, and nothing she wanted to do. Sade was a trader, an enemy, and London had only known one way to deal with an enemy. Death.

Closing the door to London's office as he walked over to where she stood placing his hand on the small of her back. London looked at him and smirked.

"What brings you by here?" she said looking at him.

"I wanted to see you," he said kissing the nape of her neck.

"This couldn't wait until tonight," she asked.

"It couldn't," he replied sliding his hands up her dress. "I wanted to talk to you about something."

"What's that?" she turned to look at him.

He scuffed, "We got a problem."

"What's the problem?"

"I might be catching a case," he said stepping away from her. "If I do end up getting bagged, I need you to do me a favor."

London leaned against her desk and looked at him. "What do you mean that you may be catching a case? How do you know this? I need you to tell me everything."

"Baby," he said grabbing her arm. "This district attorney has been coming at us hard, half of the niggas on the street are getting knocked by the boys. Trying to get them to implicate the family in something, anything."

"What do you mean?"

He looked at her and frowned. "Raven didn't tell you? This nigga was trying to get them niggas to flip on the Royals months ago. I don't know why, but this nigga has it in for the family, and it looks like he's making a career out of taking us down."

London looked at him and sighed. "What's the district attorneys name?"

"Taylor, Tyler something like that," Black asked looking at her. "Why?"

"No reason," she answered waving him off. "What do you think he knows? Do you think he knows anything?"

"Who knows? All I do know is that some of the niggas on the team are about to get indicted."

London shook her head, "What about me?"

"Nothing's on you."

London shook her head and looked at him. It was the first time since he walked through the doors that she actually looked at him.

Black didn't show any trace of him being afraid to go to jail, but what he did feel was hurt. It was as if the emotions that London had tried to keep bottled transferred onto him. From the moment the words had left his mouth that he may be going to jail, London felt as if her were world were crashing around her.

"What do you need from me?" she asked looking at him.

"Take care of everything if I do get knocked. I need you to put the family first if a nigga is looking at football numbers. I can't have you folding if I do get crossed up in this shit."

"Ok," she said shaking her head in agreement. London tried to process everything that Black had just told her as the wheels began to turn in her mind forming her own plan. A devilish grin came across her face, and she looked at Black.

"I have a meeting at three thirty," she said looking at him. "We'll talk after."

Black looked at her genuinely confused. He'd just told her that he was going to jail, and she was standing before him with a grin on her face. Pushing the thoughts that were trying to take over his mind out, he nodded his head in agreement, he stepped closer to her, leaning down and kissing her lightly on the lips. "Aight, we'll talk later. Call the girls and tell them to meet us at the house."

"I'll do that," she said.

Black walked out of the office, and London sat in her chair. She knew that everything she did from this moment would alter the course of her life, and once she crossed the line there would be no coming back. Even if she didn't want to admit it, this wasn't the legacy her parents had intended for the family, and neither had she.

When she asked the Board to give her and Black a year to make the family more viable than what it was, she didn't know that it would be this hard. In less than a year London had seen her rise, and now that she was looking at what could possibly become her fall, she decided that it was time to go against policy. Both personal and professional.

## _Chapter Fourteen_

"Normally I'd have to wait for him to be arrested before I'm able to see exactly what the charges are," Raven said as she took a sip from the glass of red wine. "But since we have a few inside men I know exactly what we're facing."

"And what is it that we're facing?" Karma asked looking at her.

Raven downed the remainder of her glass before the grabbing the bottle and refilling her cup. "Apparently everything. The district attorney has decided to keep this in house for the time being and is trusting one of the deputy's, to prosecute the cases."

"Which deputy?" London asked. "Brandon Tyler?"

Raven looked at her and frowned. "Yes, how'd you know?"

London shrugged. "When I spoke with Black earlier today, he mentioned that this attorney was hell bent on taking down the Royals," she said looking at her. "Is it true?"

Raven shook her head yes and looked from London to Karma. "Apparently he's running for District Attorney this fall, and he may be hoping that this case is what makes his career."

Karma looked at London as she moved around the kitchen. Slicing, dicing, and frying. Karma had noticed the nervous energy that exuded from her the moment they'd walked into her house.

"What's wrong with you?" Karma asked looking at her sideways.

"Nothing," London lied.

"Yeah right," Karma snapped. "Whatever it is you might as well spill it before them wild ass niggas get here."

London let out an exasperated sigh and looked at the women who were seated at the kitchen island. "I know Brandon," she said watching as their faces went through a series of contortions. "He's a client of mine."

"You knew this man and you didn't say anything?" Karma snapped.

"Listen," London said placing the knife that she was holding on the countertop. London went on to explain everything she had known about Mr. Brandon Tyler, which wasn't much.

"I don't want Black to know that I know him yet."

"London what the fuck is Black going to think? If and when that nigga goes to jail, he's going to think that you set him up to take the fall," Karma snapped.

"I know," she admitted. "But you two will be the only ones who will ever know the truth. Nothing is going on between me and Mr. Tyler."

"For now," Raven said.

London looked at both women making sure to lock eyes with them both as she continued, "Neither Black nor Vine is to know this."

"I really hope you have some kind of plan cooking up, because you are definitely playing with fire" Raven asked.

"I don't have one yet. But once I do, I'll let you know."

London began humming a tune as she went back to the business of cooking dinner for the people that were on their way to her home.

---

The sky was an ombre hue of blue and orange by the time Black pulled into his driveway. He watched the car that pulled in behind his as he placed the blunt he smoking into the ashtray.

Watching as Vine and Face stepped out of the truck, Black turned off his ignition and did the same. After leaving London's office he'd called them both and held an impromptu meeting at Harold & Belle's, a creole restaurant in south central. He informed his boys of everything he had learned when it came to the indictments over gumbo and etouffee, hoping that they'd at least be able to comfort the shit that was starting to form in his mind.

The three walked towards the front door. Black jingled his keys before placing the key into the lock opening the door. The air from the AC unit smacked him the face, as the smell of food assaulted his nostrils. Catching the tail end of the conversation the women were having Black cleared his throat before walking into the kitchen.

"Well damn," Karma said watching as the trio walked into the room. She looked at them and nodded in their direction.

"Damn," Vine said walking over towards the stove. "Had we known that you were cooking we wouldn't have stopped to get food."

"You did what?" she snapped turning from the stove to look at Black.

"I had to a nigga was craving gumbo for some reason," he said walking towards the refrigerator.

Grabbing a beer he closed the door and smacked her on the ass. "I can still eat," he said kissing her neck.

"You will," Raven mumbled under her breath sliding off the barstool. "Alright so let's get down to it."

"Aight," Vine said walking over towards the table.

"I won't know everything that we're up against until you've been arrested," Raven started. "From which point I can only represent one of you without there being a conflict of interest in the eyes of the law, if you guys end up being co-defendants."

Black shrugged. "I'm not taking my chances with nobody else," he said looking at her.

"Ok, well here's the thing I have a friend from law school, Martin Jones, he's good. I mean really good," she said looking at them. "If you don't mind, I'd like to bring him in once we get going."

"With the shit that they're trying to throw at us we gon' need a damn dream team," Face said sitting at the table. "If this punk ass DA is looking to fuck us over, aint no way in hell he'll plea us out."

"He may not have a choice," Raven said looking around the room. "If I can prove that LAPD has in some way manufactured the evidence against you and colluded with the district attorney, we can make all of it go away."

"That's a whole lot of maybe," Vine chimed in.

"Depending on the evidence, and from the previous cases I'm pretty sure a wiretap has been in place," Raven said looking around the room. "If I can prove surveillance abuse then we may have a chance."

London walked over towards the cabinet and removed the serving dishes, drowning out the people in the room. London had been in the Royal's for as long as she had been alive, and a lot of the contacts that her father had while he served as King had been passed down to London shortly after she was made Queen.

London had never disclosed information about those who actually used her firm when it came to investing funds or hiding money, and now that they were looking at a what could possibly be the unraveling of the Family she'd inherited she knew it was time to show her hand.

"Raven," London said as she began putting food into the dishes. "Here's what's going to happen. I'm going to call in a favor asking that Judge Housley oversee the cases."

"Who the fuck is that?" Black asked.

"He's on the payroll," she said in a matter of fact tone. "In fact, half of the judges in Los Angeles County are on the payroll of the family."

Everyone looked towards London and frowned. "You've been sitting on judges and we got niggas in jail?" Face asked looking at her.

"Exactly and for good reason," she said looking at them. "You don't start to call in favors until you really need them, and right now is the time to call in every favor we can."

"I can't believe this shit," Vine said looking at her. "Black hand me a beer."

Black shook his head and headed towards the fridge and grabbed Vine and Face a beer.

"What else are you holding out on?" Black asked looking at London.

"Nothing," she said a little too quick for the others in the room.

Black looked at her and made a mental note to talk to her later. London was his woman and he felt as though there was nothing that she couldn't tell him. For the rest of the evening the six people drank, smoked weed, and talked about the future of the Royal's if the men happened to fall come Monday morning.

## *Chapter Fifteen*

London had decided to go into work early the next day. After going over the logistics of the indictments with the Board and spending half the night going over why'd she hadn't told Black about the Judges that she'd known were on the Royals payroll, she needed to get out of the house.

Black had listened to London's half ass explanation knowing that she was holding back on information but didn't press her. London had waited until Black was sound asleep before leaving the house and heading towards her office. She hadn't been to sleep the night before and was riding on fumes.

There was a lot at stake. It seemed like everything around her was starting to crumble. Sade was an informant, the Senate had magically reappeared, and Black was facing jail time. Sitting at her desk trying to think of ways to save her family, when her assistant Thomas let her know that Black was on the line, she hesitated on taking the call.

She wasn't in the mood for the lecture that was sure to come. They had less than forty-eight hours to come up with a plan and hearing him complain about her leaving so early was not what she had in mind.

"Hey you," she said into the phone.

"I fucked up ma," he said in a low tone. London frowned and looked at the phone. Just as she was about to say something her cellphone chimed.

*They always say be careful what you ask for because you just might get it. According to our sources, it seems as though the King has been making more than power moves on the streets of LA. Word has gotten to us that the King has been spreading it wide and laying it low, so low that there was a recent trip to the T.H.E Clinic. Now we all know that you either go into the clinic for one of two things and being that the woman whom he was accompanying had an unmistakable baby bump we're choosing the latter. Looks like the King can no longer keep his sexual escapades under wraps. So, who is this woman? That's something we'll reveal later as the details continue to unfold. The only question on many of our minds, Where the fuck is the Queen? You'll soon hate me LA Confidential.*

Eight months ago a story like this wouldn't have caused any emotional reaction for London, because eight months ago Black meant nothing to her.

As she reread the email over and over trying to decide whether to believe the article or not, the pictures came, complete with the silence from the man on the other end of the line, London knew that there was truth behind the words written, behind the images taken. Every second that seemed to pass seemed to anger her, as Black refused to say anything. Other than his breathing on the line she wouldn't have known that he was still there.

"Is it true?" she asked. Her tone even and masking the hurt that she was feeling.

"Can you meet for lunch?"

"Is it true?" she asked again. No longer able to contain the single tear that fell from her eyes. As quickly as it fell her hand wiped it away.

"Part of it," he said into the phone letting out a sigh. "Meet me for lunch."

"I can't," she replied. "I have a meeting in an hour. We'll talk later."

London hung up the phone before she could hear his reply. She looked down at her cellphone, as Karma's name and number sprawled across the screen. Declining the call she placed her cell on the desk.

"Ms. Clark," Thomas's voice boomed through the intercom. "Karma's on line one, Raven's on two, also Mr. Harrison is on five."

"Put Karma through," she responded.

"London," Karma's voice boomed through the speaker. "Please tell me Black's ok."

London chuckled. "Wow. I'm the bitch being played, and you're worried about that nigga," London scuffed.

"You know what the fuck I mean," Karma said.

"No I don't," London snapped. "But yeah he's ok."

Karma sighed. "You know how this site be twisting shit around. Black couldn't have been fucking with another bitch, London. You and I both know that nigga loves you more than anyone else in this world."

"That may be true, but love aint never stopped any of these niggas from fucking around with another bitch."

"True, but Black's not like that," Karma defended.

"And how the fuck would you know? The nigga called me on some 'ma I fucked up' type shit and you're going to tell me that the nigga aint like that," London screamed into the phone.

Both were silent for a moment. Karma knew that London was hurt, it was evident. She would've been hurt too had the site pulled up some stuff on Vine, so she couldn't fault her for being pissed. Karma also knew that London loved Black, wholeheartedly and would die if that nigga told her to. London had given Black every part of her, and in return the gossip site had ammo to burn down the house that London built with him.

Over the past eight months London had lost both parents, most of the people she had trusted for as long as she could remember, and now she was on the verge of losing the only thing that was keeping her sane, Black.

"What'd he say?" Karma asked.

"Nothing, just that he fucked up."

"Raven's calling on the other line. Do you want me to patch her in?"

"It really doesn't matter at this point does it, because you're already dialing her damn number," London said as she listened to the keys being pressed on the other end.

"Hold on," she said clicking over.

London looked down at her cell as it began to vibrate.

*I need to talk to you. Answer the phone- Black*

*I'm fine, Andre. I'll see you when I get home. -London*

*So I'm Andre now??? I wanna talk to you so you can know what's real and what's not. -Black*

*We'll talk later. I'm not responding anymore. Handle your business and I'll see you tonight. -London*

"London," Karma said coming back on the line. "Raven?"

"Yes," they said in unison.

"London are you ok? What the fuck is going on? Who is this bitch? You know we can go to this bitch house and beat the fuck out of her and whoever else," Raven said into the phone.

"I'm fine," London responded in a calm tone.

"Yeah too damn fine if you ask me," Karma snapped. "London if you're pissed say that shit so we can know what the move is. Are we killing Black? Are we killing this bitch? Are we burning down the house? Bitch just tell us what you need us to do."

"Get my shit from Black's house," she responded.

"Ok that we can do," Raven responded. "You sure you don't wanna go beat this bitch ass?"

"No. I got other shit to do," she said looking at the clock that hung on the wall. "I'm not doing this shit no more. Why is it that every time I get with a nigga he always has to be on some bogus shit? Why can't I ever find someone that's on the up and up?"

"You want the truth, or you want me to lie to you," Karma asked.

"The truth."

"Look at the circles we run in. All we know is these types of niggas," Karma said. "Most times you'll get a nigga that's really about you, and then other times-"

"You end up with the Pick's, Don's and Black's of the world," London finished.

"Exactly."

"Karma you mind if I stay with you for a few days until I find a place," London asked.

"You know I got you."

"Aight. I need y'all to go get my shit from this niggas house. I'm not going back there at all."

"Damn one and done," Raven said.

"I'm not giving him the opportunity to keep doing me dirty, bitch I'm about to be twenty-six, and this is not the shit I plan on doing for the rest of my life," London capped.

"I hear you," Raven agreed.

"Just go get my stuff, and Karma I'll see you later," London said ending the call.

Looking down at her cell she read the messages that Black continued to send. She pressed the button turning her phone off and threw it into her desk.

"London," Thomas came over the intercom.

"Yes."

"Mr. Tyler is here to see you."

"I'll be out in a moment."

---

Black sat in the passenger seat of Face's Cadillac truck smoking a blunt. He kept dialing London's number but to no avail she wouldn't answer. Black knew that he had fucked up in a major way, and he didn't know what was going to come of the situation. He was more pissed at the gossip site for breaking the news instead of himself, for even being in the situation in the first place.

Thinking that Monica wouldn't be stupid enough to keep a baby by a nigga that she wasn't with. Not only had Monica planned on keeping the baby, she was telling anyone who would listen that he was the child's father.

Black knew that it was only a matter of time before word got back to London, and he knew once it did that she would be pissed. He needed her to be pissed, but instead London was calm. Too damn calm. If there was one thing he knew, especially being raised by a black woman. That when a woman was calm your whole world was about to collapse.

London had stopped responding to his text messages and turned off her cellphone. When he called the office her assistant would send him to her voicemail. Hoping that the blunt filled with haze would take away the feelings that were starting to succumb him.

He looked out the window as Face drove around the city. They had no destination, and no work to really handle for the day, so they were out without a cause.

"You need to stop thinking about that shit," Face said breaking the silence. "London can't be that mad my nigga. She knows that shit happens."

"Shit aint supposed to happen," Black said taking a deep pull from the blunt. "If this damn site wasn't up, I would be able to explain this shit. But she heard this shit from someone other than me."

Face sighed. "You're thinking too hard on that shit."

"You just don't know."

Face looked over at Black and shook his head. It was the first time he had ever seen his cousin trip behind some pussy, so he knew that the feelings Black had for London were deep. He had been around both of them enough to know that the love they had for each other was genuine, and rare.

But as he looked at his boy, he needed the nigga to snap out of it. Although London and Black were betrothed to one another, Face didn't think that it honestly meant that they were supposed to be together.

Like every nigga in the game, shit happens. Whether its jail, or other bitches, shit happens, and for Face, if London couldn't handle the little shit. She damn sure wouldn't be able to handle big shit. True he knew that London was a rider, manipulator, and the Queen of his 'world' but London was a woman, and she was a woman that needed to know her place.

"What don't I know?" he said as he made a left on Imperial.

"London, cuz. She been through enough shit with niggas, and now here it is some shit that I'm pulling. She might leave me."

"Nigga she aint going nowhere," Face said with a hearty laugh. Black was in his feelings and he couldn't help but to laugh at his young pup.

Black looked down at his cell and frowned. "Take me to the house cuz," he seethed.

"What's wrong now?"

"Vine just texted and said that London is sending Karma and Raven for her shit."

Face looked at him to see if he were joking. When he didn't see a trace of a smirk, only a scowl as water welled in his eyes.

'Damn. We need to find the bitch that's behind this site. I'd be damned if I'm looking like this nigga thanks to an internet thug,' Face thought as he maneuvered several lanes pulling onto the freeway.

## *Chapter Sixteen*

Karma had made it to Black's house in record timing. No sooner than she had pulled into the driveway and turned off the ignition, Face's truck pulled next to her car. She and Raven watched as Black hopped out of the truck before it could come to a complete stop and stalked over towards her car.

Karma immediately regretted calling Vine to let him know that she was going to Black's house to get London's things, at the time she just wanted to know where he kept a spare key, but now as she watched the man of the hour staring at her through her windshield she was at a loss.

Raven's hand absently found its way to the switch on the door panel for the locks of Karma's car, locking the doors. The look that was plastered across his face caused her heart to sink in the pit of her stomach. The look on his face displayed one emotion, pain. Black was hurt, more than either of them could've imagined.

His face displayed his regrets, and Raven genuinely felt for him. Looking at his low eyes thanks to the blunt that he smoked, Raven could still see the tears that formed in his eyes threatening to fall. His usually put together appearance was less than. Dressed in a Nike sweat suit and matching sneakers, and the only jewelry he wore was a gold Rolex, and a diamond stud in his ear.

"I'm not getting out this car bitch," Raven whispered as if he could hear her.

"Bitch me either," Karma agreed. "Look at him. That nigga is hurt, and you know hurt dogs always bite, and I'd be damn if he bites my head off because he can't get to London."

"Then what the fuck are we going to do? London needs her shit out of this house."

"Hell if I know," Karma said looking at her. "That nigga is looking at us like he wants to beat the fuck out of us. Like we're the ones who did this shit to him."

Tap. Tap. Tap.

"Karma roll down the window," Black demanded as he knelt down looking at both of them.

"You good?" Karma asked through the closed window.

"Yeah ma, I'm good. Just roll down the window."

"Bitch you a fool if you roll down the window," Raven said as Karma pressed her finger on the button lowering the window to a crack.

Running his hands over his face, he looked at the women inside of the car. "I fucked up," he said in a low tone. "I can admit that shit."

"Black-" Karma started but the look on his face silenced her.

"I can't let you take my bitch up out of here," he said looking at her. "Tell her ass to come home so we can work this shit out."

"Black you know how London is. You've been around her ass every day for a while now. Once she makes up her mind to do something that's what it is," Karma said looking from him to Raven.

"She won't even let me explain," he said looking at her. "She turned off the phone, she won't answer at the office."

"Then give her ass some time," Raven said causing him to look directly at her.

"How much time am I supposed to give her?" he asked.

"A few days," Raven said.

"She'll be at my house," Karma said. "You know you can come over and talk to her."

"Fuck," he yelled as he rested his head on the door. "She can't leave me cuz."

Karma looked at him and frowned. "Nigga get a grip," Karma said with an attitude. "The bitch just needs a few days. She didn't say that she was leaving yo black ass."

Both Black and Raven looked at Karma shocked. "Move," she said looking at him as she opened the car door and slamming it shut. "Now give me the keys so I can go get my cousin some clothes for the next few days."

Black stood up and looked down at Karma's five feet three-inch frame. Reaching into his pocket and removing his keys he handed them to her and watched as she switched her short ass away and headed towards the house.

Black looked over at Face who was smiling like the cat who ate the canary, before bursting out in laughter. What Karma lacked in height she damn sure made up for in heart. It wasn't a nigga dead or alive who could talk to Black like she had and get away with it. He had to give it to her she was down for her cousin and didn't give a damn if he cried a river, she was not going against the mission she was set out to complete.

"You just keep getting it today aint you my nigga," Face joked.

Black flipped him off and knelt down and looked at Raven. Noticing that she had traded in her normal wears for jeans, an oversized shirt, and sneakers. He chuckled to himself and shook his head.

"Who ass was you coming to beat?" he asked between laughing.

"Yours if you were on some hoe shit," she capped.

"I don't want no beef with y'all," he admitted.

"I hope not," Raven said looking at him. "Because if you think London is crazy. Imagine the bitches that she fucks with."

Raven opened the door and stepped from the car. She looked over at Face and smirked.

"And yo ass," she said pointing a finger in his direction. "I heard about the hoe shit you did to Tiffany. If her ass wasn't so damn dick whipped, we'd be doing this shit at yo house too."

"When you come to take her ass out my house make sure you keep her ass too?" Face laughed.

Raven shook her head as she watched Karma return with two Louis Vuitton duffel bags in her hands.

"I thought you said a few days," Black said with a confused look on her face.

"Damn the bitch do need to wash her ass don't she," Karma snapped as she threw the bags into the backseat. She turned and looked at Black and shook her head.

'Two dumb asses in love,' she thought.

"Listen," she started. "Come through whenever to talk to London. But just know this shit aint gon be easy at all. You fucked up bad my nigga. A whole fucking baby, meanwhile, your girl is thinking that you are taking care of business. The shit perplexes me."

"The shit perplexes me too," Raven said. "If, and I do mean if, London forgives you after this shit. Just know that even the devil himself aint gon be able to save yo ass from that crazy bitch."

Black sighed as the women got in Karma's car and pulled out of the driveway. Black looked over at Face and frowned.

"I want the bitch that's behind that site."

# *Chapter Seventeen*

The sounds coming from the outside of the house caused him to awake with a start. Sitting up in his bed he listened as the sounds seemed to grow louder with every breath that he took. Standing from the bed he walked over towards the chair that sat in the corner removing the jeans that were on them and putting them on. No sooner had he pulled his jeans up and buckled them, the crashing sound coming from downstairs caught his attention.

Walking back towards his bed, Black took a seat as he listened to door after door of his home being opened, followed by the bass of one voice yelling "Clear".

A part of him was glad that London hadn't been at the house for what was happening. She was the only one who was clean of the shit that was going down within the family, and her getting caught up in a raid wouldn't have looked good.

When his bedroom door smashed open, six red dots covered his body, mainly aimed at his torso. As he looked at the men holding the guns, trained on him a devilish smirk came to his face.

"Down…down…down," the commands came. "Get the fuck on the ground."

Black raised his hands in the air and did as he was told, lying on the floor face down, palms up. It felt like every one of the officers had jumped on his body as they placed the handcuffs on him, yanked him to his feet, and escorted him down the stairs. He watched helplessly as the officers ran in and out of his house, gathering 'evidence'.

Black knew that there was nothing in his home. No guns, drugs, money. He never brought anything home with him, and whatever evidence they claimed to find in his home wouldn't be much to hold him on unless it were planted. Being that it was LAPD making the arrest anything was possible.

Black had spent the past seventy-two hours preparing for this moment. He'd given Monica more money than she'd ever know what to do with to take care of their child while he was away, even though he hoped for no more than a few days, majority of the money he'd had stashed at safe houses he'd moved to an undisclosed location giving only his mother the intel just in case London couldn't come through on her end of the plan.

He'd only hoped that by the time he made it to the precinct and was booked that the women he left with his life in their hands would be coming through with the news he needed to hear.

---

"Turn to your right," the officer called out. He stared at the chubby man, and grimaced. His large potbelly overlapped his standard issued officer blue pants, off yellow teeth that protruded through his mouth causing it to remain open long after he had finished speaking.

Taking his eyes off the man, Black did as he was instructed. Before he could blink the picture was taken, and he was escorted to a holding cell, until his arraignment. The guard closed the iron bars and the loud thud indicating that the bars were indeed locked, he looked around the room and chuckled.

Face, Vine, TG, Stuck, and himself had all been involved in the bust and as he walked over towards the two benches that the men occupied, he slapped hands with them all before taking a seat.

Black had heard many sordid tales about holding cells at police precincts and being that he had never seen the inside of one in his endeavors, Black looked around in disdain. He had known that it would've only been a matter of time before he had gotten crossed up in the penal system, but he had no idea that it would come nine months into his life as King of the Royals.

The members of his crew were sitting right beside him, and it infuriated him even more. He had to give it to the cops, not only had they managed to arrest the Board of the Royals, but they arrested all of them simultaneously.

"When'd they get y'all?" Black asked looking around the room.

"I got here last night," Stuck answered. "Then every hour on the hour one of you niggas rolled in here."

"You got a lawyer?" Vine asked him.

"Nah," he answered in a defeated tone. "I'll probably roll with a public defender a nigga can't afford to go broke fucking with a lawyer."

TG was holding the paperwork he'd requested from one of the officers reading the papers over and over.

"With the shit they charging us with nigga I suggest yo cheap ass hire a fucking lawyer," he said handing Stuck the paperwork. "When you talk to your girl, have her ass hook me up with someone that can get this shit wiped away."

"I got you," Black said looking at him.

"What's this shit about surveillance audio with confirmed transactions about drug shipments?" Stuck said handing the paperwork to Black. "We stopped talking on the phones after the first raid."

Black looked down at the paperwork as the sounds of footsteps, and keys jingling could be heard coming down the hall. Reading over the paperwork quickly he passed them to Vine, who did the same.

"Terrance Gregory," the officer yelled.

TG looked around the room and stood to his feet.

"You've made bail."

The looks that were plastered across the men's faces spoke volumes. As TG looked at them, he swallowed hard before being escorted out of the holding cell. Black shook his head and looked at the remaining members of his crew.

"That nigga turned," Stuck said his voice dripping with disdain.

"Aint none of us got bail," Face said looking around the room. "How the fuck that nigga get bail?"

"He working," Black said letting out an exasperated sigh. "I need Raven to pull up like now. I need that nigga got."

"Say less my nigga," Vine said. "That nigga will be taken care of before the end of the day."

Black looked at him and shook his head in agreement. Vine handed him the papers and Black continued to read what he already had known to be true. Looking around the cell he noticed that not one other person had been given the paperwork involving their cases, only TG had.

As bad as he didn't want to accept the fact that his day one had turned state's witness against the rest of him, he couldn't go against what he knew to be true.

"Stuck," Black said looking at him. "Have you had your phone call?"

"Yea I called my girl and told her that I was being held at 77th until court."

"Aight," he said. "When Raven gets down here, I'll tell her what to do in regard to this nigga TG. That nigga is not to make it to court."

The men shook their heads in agreement, as they all sat back engulfed in their own thoughts. Black had only hoped that the girls would be able to pull off everything he needed down.

There was already a contingency plan in effect, as they had known that someone within the organization had been talking, and now that they knew who the person was Black needed the girls to handle their part of the deal. All he knew was, TG was not to make it to court or else they were fucked.

---

Karma watched as London paced the floor of her living room ranting and raving about what they'd all knew was going to happen three days ago. Listening to her cousin go on about how they'd all fucked up, as she sipped her coffee, Karma was increasingly losing her patience.

She wanted to grab the woman and tell her that everything that was happening was mainly her fault. Had she not been so hell bent on getting rid of those she considered disloyal to the Family she would've been prepared for this moment. Instead of Karma speaking her mind she shook her head in agreement whenever the opportunity presented itself during the thirty minutes London had spent going off the rails.

"Did you call the judge to see if he's the presiding over the case?" Karma asked while taking a sip from her cup.

"Yes," London said letting out a sigh. "He wants one hundred thousand per case."

"Okay," Karma said looking at her confused. "So pay the man and get them out."

London stopped pacing for a moment and looked at her. "I don't think I should."

"What the fuck are you talking about? You know just like I do that if those niggas have to stay in jail, they're going to blame you, and then shit is really going to go left."

London waved her off. "I'm not talking about Vine and Face if that's what you're worried about."

"Black? You're thinking about leaving Black in jail. London what the fuck is going on with you," Karma asked staring at her as if she had completely lost her mind.

"No, but I don't need him coming after me."

"Coming after you for what?" Karma asked looking at her. "What is it that you plan on doing?"

London sighed and looked at her. "I think I might start dating Brandon."

Karma took a sip from her coffee and motioned with her hand for London to continue. She needed to know the plan full out if she were going to follow her and the ingenious plan that she had conjured up.

"Black has some kind of hold on my soul, and in order for this shit to work the way I need it to then I have to leave Black completely."

"What are you saying?"

"I'm saying that it's over. I'm done with Black."

"What about the family?"

"I'm going to split the family. Black will still take care of the shit that he needs to take care of, and I'll still do my part, but as far as Black and I coming within fifteen feet of each other. That's out. I may even have to stop fucking with y'all for a while," she said taking a seat on the couch.

"London," Karma said looking at her. "I know you have a plan, and right now you're the only one who knows how it'll work out. I need you to be completely sure that this is what you really want to do."

London was silent for a while as she thought about her options. Sure London hadn't thought the plan out in its entirety and now that she and Karma were talking about it out loud she knew that the only way for the plan to work out the way she had intended for it to, she would have to cut off everyone including her girls.

"Give me some time and you'll see that this is what's best for the family. I can't have the family go down like this. We have people talking to the boys in blue about us, and we're not any closer to leading this family to where we need it to be."

"We all knew that when the ranks shifted that shit would go left," Karma started. "This is the life. Shit happens all the time."

"Yeah well we're about to become non-existent in a minute," London snapped. "We all fucked up. I thought that this would be a walk in the park and so far, it hasn't been. In order to save this family I have to do this. I have to take Brandon up on his offer."

London looked at Karma with tears in her eyes as she grabbed her purse and walked out of her house. Karma didn't know what to make of what had just happened, but she knew that London's mind was made up and there was no changing it. Never would she imagine the length that London was willing to take to protect the Royals.

# *Chapter Eighteen*

The soothing sounds of Ron Isley crooning the lyrics of, Voyage to Atlantis, filled the house blasting from the stereo system. Other than the light coming from the eighty-inch flatscreen that hung on the wall no lights were on in the house. The tv played Game 1 of the NBA Finals with the sound on mute. Sitting on the couch smoking a blunt as the game went into the third quarter, he half watched the game, even though he had a five thousand dollar bet with his boy Stuck on the game.

Listening intently as the words of the song playing danced around in his head.

"I'll always come back to you," he sang along to the lyrics. Tapping his feet and nodding his head to the rhythm, he grabbed the remote for the stereo starting the song over and turning up the volume.

Sixteen days, eighteen hours, and forty minutes had passed since the last time he had saw or spoken to London. She wouldn't answer his calls, and the gifts that he'd send to her office were always returned unopened. He'd even dropped by Karma's a few times hoping to catch her, but after the fifth time Karma had informed him that London had only stayed with her a few nights before moving into a townhouse in Manhattan Beach.

To say that Black was losing his mind would've been an understatement. After Raven had managed to get him released on bail, he didn't leave the house unless it were for food, weed, or liquor. No moves were made on his behalf while he'd been held in the house, listening to oldies, smoking weed, chain smoking cigarettes, and wondering where the hell London was and who she was doing it with seemed to be his only concern.

Black just wanted the chance to explain. True, there would never be an explanation when it came to him having a child outside of their relationship, but he needed London to know that the lapse in judgement was just that, a lapse in judgement. Knowing everything that she had been through with men made the ordeal that much harder.

He knew that it wouldn't be easy for London to forgive him, and he knew that he would have to jump through several hoops before she'd give him another chance to play with her heart, but what he didn't expect was the silence. He knew how to handle the situation if she'd just talk to him, but the silence was louder than any other sound he had ever heard.

Never had a woman made him feel the way he was feeling at this moment. No woman had ever been able to say that she had him caught out there, and now that London had him in his body, the feelings that were taking over were unfamiliar and unwelcomed. Black was a street nigga through and through, and he knew the game when it came to women, but he had never played the game that London was playing. She was winning and even if he did want to even the score he couldn't and wouldn't. He wanted his woman home where she belonged.

After a week of no word from London, he'd cut Monica off completely. Other than doctor visits and checking on his unborn child he rarely spoke to the woman. He wanted to blame Monica entirely for the situation that he was in, but he couldn't. She didn't have a responsibility to London only he did. In his selfish mind she could've gotten rid of the baby, and then his life with London would still be in existence.

As the song started over for the tenth time that night, he rested his head on the back of the couch thinking of ways to get his girl back.

The jingling of keys could be heard through the closed front door, grabbing the remote to turn down the volume his front door opened, and there she was flanked by Karma and Raven. London waved at the cloud of smoke that began exiting the house and looked around in disgust. His eyes following hers.

Empty liquor bottles, overflowing ashtrays, old boxes of pizza and fast food wrappings were strewn around the place letting off a stench as soon as you entered the house. Black hadn't bothered to clean the house, take out the trash, or even shave. As London's eyes landed on him, she shook her head and climbed the stairs.

"Hey," Raven and Karma said in unison as they followed her.

Black watched as the three women climbed his stairs, disappearing from sight. With the lights coming on upstairs and the sounds of the doors opening to the rooms, panic set in. She was leaving him. Black stood to his feet and climbed the stairs taking two at a time.

Making it to the top he watched as London moved through the rooms, telling her girls what to grab, and handing them duffel bags to fill with her belongings. London moved past him never once looking in his direction as she made her way towards the master bedroom.

"Can we talk?" he asked following behind her. Black followed her into the bedroom and closed the door.

"I'm not really in the mood," she said walking into the closet. "I just want to get my things and go home."

"Ma," he said walking behind her. "Baby I'm sorry. I know I fucked up-"

London turned around and looked at him, before Black could finish his sentence London slapped the shit out of him. The sounds echoed throughout the master suite, and from the hurried footsteps that were coming down the hall she knew that her girls had heard the slap through the closed door.

"Don't do that," she screamed. "Don't make it seem like I did this shit to you. You got a bitch pregnant."

"I didn't mean-" he started but was cut off.

"Y'all niggas never mean to do shit. Y'all don't ever mean for shit to happen like this," she snapped raising her hand to slap him again.

The look that came over his face let her know that if she touched him again it would be the last thing she did. London shook her head and pushed past him.

"I fucked up. I've apologized a thousand fucking times. What more do you want from me?" he said in a low tone.

"To leave me alone," she said as she began pulling down hangers of her clothes.

Black grabbed her arm, snapping her around to face him. "You can't leave me."

He grabbed her by the forearm, pushing her against the plexiglass shoe boxes.

"Move," she said as she tried to break free from his grasp.

He leaned down, running his lips from her cheek to her neck. London scuffed, as she continued to try to break free. The hold that he had on her arms wouldn't allow her to move his hand.

"Please," she said trying to avoid his kisses. She could feel Black using his knee to push her legs apart. London immediately regretted the knee length summer dress that she was wearing, as her legs opened.

"I'm not doing this with you today," she said.

Black leaned over, the hairs from his beard running along her neck as he kissed her gently. "I need you," he said between kisses. "I can't let you leave."

"You don't have a choice," she said closing her eyes. London moved her head slightly giving him a better angle of her neck.

Black looked down at her before kissing her lips. A moan escaped her lips as she braced for what was to come.

'Don't be a weak bitch,' her subconscious screamed. 'Don't let him get the best of you. He fucked up.'

Black released the grip he had on her arms, and London wrapped her arms around his neck pulling him closer. Placing his hands under her dress gently palming her ass, before lifting her up.

Wrapping her legs around his waist London used one of her hands to reach down into his sweats releasing his dick from the cotton fabric that held his erect member hostage. Carrying her over towards the bed, he lay her down, reaching under her dress removing her panties. Taking a look at her neatly shaved box, his dick jumped as he leaned on top of her placing his member at her entrance, penetrating her.

Black closed his eyes for a moment as he relished in the moment, letting her tightness wrap around his member before slowly stroking her. A moan escaped her lips as she pulled the dress over her head tossing it on the other end of the room.

'Stupid bitch,' she thought as he began stroking her in a way that only he knew how.

After going at it for twenty minutes, London watched as he lay next to her on the bed looking at the ceiling. Sliding out of the bed and walking into the bathroom turning on the shower, London stepped into the hot water. Washing her body as quickly as she could, before returning to the room and heading for the closet.

Black watched as she slipped into a pair of sweats and a t-shirt. "What you doing?"

"Can I borrow the two duffels that's in here?" she called to him.

"What for?" he asked confused.

London turned and looked at him. "I'm still leaving," she said with a frown on her face. "Sex doesn't fix shit that's going on with us."

"So what can I do to fix this London?" he asked standing to his feet.

She shrugged. "I don't know. All I know is I can't live here. I don't know if you fucked that bitch in this bed, in this house," she said shaking her head as the thought of him sleeping with another woman in the bed they shared came to mind. "I can't live in the same house with you right now."

"So what're you saying? You done?"

"I don't know," she answered honestly.

Black walked over to where she stood and pulled her close to him. "Come on ma. We can get through this shit."

A slight chuckle left her. "You want this," she said moving her hand between the two of them. "Then work for it."

London moved away from him and walked out of the room leaving him alone. She could be heard telling her girls something which he couldn't make out, followed by the front door closing. Black didn't know what to do. He knew that he needed to give London her space, and in the meantime, he was going to get his shit together.

As he stepped into his bathroom looking into the mirror one thing was certain. With the summer coming to an end, he was feeling the effects of a man who was had just about lost everything. Leaving him with one thing in mind, everything and everyone was now, food.

London pulled out of Black's driveway damn near hitting his car and a few others, as she peeled off the block.

"Damn London," Karma said as London made a hard right off the block. "Don't kill us in this damn car. Aint shit in the rule book that says I have to die with you two bitches."

"Shut up," London snapped coming to a stop sign. "I wasn't going to kill you. I just needed to get out of there."

"The way you were screaming that niggas name," Raven said from the backseat. "I didn't know if you were staying or going."

"Please," London said looking in the rearview mirror. "Just because we had sex doesn't mean shit."

"I know that's right," Karma said looking at her.

London smirked as she looked at Raven in the backseat and laughed lightly noticing that she was holding onto the hanger rack in the backseat. "I can't front, it was good. Real good."

"So why the fuck are we moving you out?" Karma asked looking at her.

London sighed. "Because Black fucked up. Sleeping with another bitch is one thing, I can handle that, but a baby is another. How the hell am I supposed to compete with that?"

"You can't," Raven said. "And nobody asked you to compete with a baby."

London let out an exasperated sigh as she maneuvered through the nights traffic.

"I know but that's just what it is. I'll be competing with a kid that's not mine. You know how bitches are once they have a niggas baby. Them bitches automatically think that they have some kind of claim to the nigga just because they his kid," London said.

"Yea but you know Black wouldn't even put-" Karma stopped talking.

London sighed as she turned up the radio of the car, letting the music drown out her girls and fill her thoughts. She'd had one mission in mind that night, go and get her belongings. She hadn't intended on seeing Black nor sleeping with him. In fact she expected him to be gone, giving her the chance to be in and out before he even knew she'd come and gone.

After icing him out for over two weeks, she didn't know what to expect when she walked through the door. She knew that Black would be a mess, Karma had told her about the way he looked when he dropped by her house, but she didn't expect him to look like he had. Black was a mess. He looked as though he hadn't shaved or had a decent haircut since the day they talked. Black had neglected the house as well, giving her the impression that he was in deep.

London loved Black and she knew that he loved her, but there were some things that London would no longer accept. She had been through hell with men, and Black had heard every sordid tale, so she didn't expect him to do the same thing to her.

London had even thought about going home, and after the first few days at Karma's she had all but packed her bags ready to return home to Black, especially after Vine and Face tried to plead his case. But as the days went by London had gone from distraught about her current situation to plain out pissed.

The feelings that she tried hard to suppress over the past two weeks seemed to come rushing back, and after letting Black enter her treasure box things were even more complicated. At least for her.

"I hate that he did this to us," she said turning onto her block.

Karma looked over at London and then towards the backseat at Raven. "You need to talk to that nigga then. At least hear him out, and then set some kind of boundaries."

"Exactly. We all know that you don't want to leave him, so fix the shit already," Raven chimed in.

"It's not that easy," London said as she reached into the center console and handed Karma her phone.

"What do you want me to do with this?" Karma said looking at her phone.

"I started receiving personal emails from the site about a week ago," she said.

London looked over and watched as Karma opened the home screen and went to London's emails. Karma watched as dozens of text messages appeared on London's screen. As she read every one her heart ached for her cousin.

The site had every text that Black had made to the mystery woman carrying his child, dating back to the night Black was made King of the Royal's. Every single word was there in black and white, and as Karma's eyes landed on the ones that came just a month ago, she wanted to cry. Black had told the woman he loved her, and that once she had the baby, he'd make sure that her and the baby got the family they needed.

London pulled into her driveway and turned off the ignition. Karma let out an exasperated sigh and passed the phone to Raven. Raven began reading the messages and looked at London. They all were silent, waiting for someone to break the silence.

"He loves her," London said as a tear fell from her eyes. London wiped the tear away. "The messages may have come from a bogus phone, but who's to say."

"We're going to find out," Raven said placing her hand on her shoulder.

"There's no need. I don't even want to know if they're real or fake," she said looking out the window. "We still have to run the family together, and before shit goes back to being fucked up this issue needs to be dead. I'm no longer giving this anymore energy."

Raven and Karma shook their head in agreement. "Okay," Karma said looking at her. "So what's the next move?"

London shrugged. "Call a meeting with the Board."

"You know it's just us and them," Raven said sitting up in her seat.

"I know," she said opening her door. "We're taking a vote."

"On what?"

"Splitting the family," London answered stepping out of the car.

# *Chapter Nineteen*

Raven pulled into the available space in front of Karma's store. Normally she would've met her at her house, but after the day she'd had in court, waiting on Karma to come to her wasn't an option.

Raven had managed to get most of her clients deals with the State or released on bail. The ones who were still in jail took their deals after agreeing that the Royal's would take care of their families while they were away. Although the task was to get them off, Raven knew that with the priors that her clients had on their record there was no way the District Attorney would've let them walk away scot free, so plea deals were the next best thing.

Looking around the crowded street with its many storefront properties, Raven turned off her ignition and opened the car door letting the summer heat attack her being. Karma's store, Off-Rodeo, was located on Market

Street. One of the busiest streets in Inglewood. The locals who patronized the local shops in search of clothes, shoes, and jewelry, and good food seemed to keep Karma's store afloat. The smell of food assaulted Raven's nostrils, thanks to the soul food restaurants scattered throughout the three blocks that made up the square, causing her stomach to growl. Raven realized that she hadn't eaten all day and was famished.

Stepping out of her car and pressing the alarm she headed towards Karma's store. While her stores catered to the women who couldn't afford the designer labels, they craved on a nine to five income and welfare check alone, Karma damn sure didn't wear the wares she sold. Knock off Gucci, Prada, Chanel, Balenciaga filled the stores, Raven had to admit that whoever Karma got her product from they were definitely top-notch. The stitching was perfect on every piece of material and matched the original designs down to the tags. Each of Karma's stores had been decorated to resemble the boutiques that they'd frequent, giving women in the surrounding area a sense of the Rodeo shops while they shopped.

Walking through the glass paneled doors, Raven looked around the store. The walls had been painted white with a silver borders, plush rugs scattered throughout the space surrounded by coffee tables that held magazines atop, and white plush Italian leather chairs, crystal chandeliers hung from the ceilings, several winter white drapes hung over the back wall and were tied on either side, leading towards the dressing room.

Karma had spent a pretty penny on decorating the place, and from the looks of the women who still in the store waiting to be rung up, Raven knew that she was more than making her money back in sales. Looking down at the watch on her wrist, it was closing in on six-thirty, and other than the few customers and two employees that were in the front the store was empty.

"Is Karma here?" Raven asked walking over towards one of the white chairs taking a seat.

"Yea," one of them turned around and said. "She's in the back. I'll get her."

Raven watched as the woman disappeared and reached into her purse removing her cell. She looked down at the screen and shook her head as she read the email that was sprawled across it.

*This just in: It seems as though our Queen has been spotted with a man other than the King, and from a reliable source we're confident in saying that it's Los Angeles's own newly appointed District Attorney. That's right folks, the very one who prosecuted the cases of the Royal's. Word is they've been together for a little under six months, and have yet to go public with their relationship, at least to the ones that matter. We wonder if like us, the Royal's have been caught blindsided by the apparent betrayal... Don't worry we'll be here to detail the blow back that's sure to come. Soon you'll hate me, LA Confidential.*

Raven threw her phone back into her purse and leaned back in her seat. The person behind the site had seemed to become more of a nuisance lately, and it was starting to become a pain in her ass. They'd all tried desperately to find the person that was behind the site, but they'd all come back empty. The site had been routed through several countries and was seemingly untraceable. There was nothing that any of them could do when it came to the thug who sat behind the confines of a computer screen telling any and everything they knew.

"Tell me you read that email," Karma said coming from the back of the store.

"Oh, I read it," she said looking at her. "The question is, has Black read it?"

"Damn," Karma said looking at her. "I wonder why she aint called me. We were all supposed to meet up for dinner tonight, right?"

"Yea," Raven said still looking at the woman. "But you know how that shit goes. Whenever we're supposed to meet up, she suddenly has something else to do. Ever since she got with that dude it's been one thing after the next."

"You know she's only doing this to save us all, right?" Karma said looking at her.

"That's what she said, and it's what I used to believe. But I think London has forgotten the plan. I think she may genuinely be in love with him."

Karma waved her off. "I doubt it. Black still holds the key to her soul."

"That niggas gonna be holding more than her soul if she doesn't surface soon," Raven said.

"I didn't even think about that," Karma admitted. "Black's going to kill her if he thinks that she crossed him and the family for this dude."

"We," Raven said waving her finger between the two of them. "Know that London is doing this for him, but that nigga will not see it like that at all."

"I know. He's been in and out of court for the past three months trying to fight this damn case."

"Exactly, and while he's becoming frustrated by the delay of the trial. He's becoming paranoid since he hasn't spoken to London since they all got arrested three months ago."

"You talked to Sade?" Karma asked changing the subject.

"Not since yesterday," she said with a frown. "I really don't feel like hanging with her ass tonight. I'm not in the mood to be playing twenty-one questions. I have a headache, I need a drink, and I got plans tonight."

"Plans," Karma said looking at her. "What plans?"

Raven looked at the woman across the room and smirked before standing to her feet. "Don't be all in my shit."

"What I tell you about fucking the bitches that work for me? That's why I had to fire the last two," Karma joked. She walked towards the back of the store and came back within moments carrying her purse.

"Let's go," she said to Raven. "Aight I'm out. Don't forget to lock up and make that drop tonight."

"Alright," the girls said in unison as the women walked out of the store.

Stepping into Raven's car, Karma turned and looked at her. "Did you get that thing we talked about?"

Raven reached into the backseat, retrieving a box and handing it to her. "It's supposed to kill transmissions within a ten-mile radius."

"You sure this'll work," Karma asked opening the box.

Raven started the car and pulled out of the spot. "If not we'll all be in jail come the new year."

"Don't even joke like that," Karma snapped. Although she knew Raven were only joking, she knew that things between Sade and the rest of the girls had drastically changed, and they would never go back to what they once were.

Black had finally let them know that it was time to take care of Sade. He had known her comings and goings for over a year and had enough information on the woman to hire a team of killers to go after the woman, but he hadn't. Not only had Raven's instincts been correct when it came to Sade wearing a wire, but it seemed as though she was working privately with federal agents to get her parents sentences reduced.

Although the girls knew that Sade couldn't have any information on the Royal's it didn't stop Black from delivering an ultimatum. Sade was a problem, and they couldn't afford the kind of liability that came in the form of Sade. Leaving the task to the girls.

With London running around playing house with the district attorney all in the name of protecting the family, and with Raven breaking laws left and right as the family's attorney, leaving Karma to fulfill the task at hand. Other than fucking Vine, she hadn't done a thing. She collected money, hid money here and there, but she wasn't really taking as much of a gamble as her counterparts.

No one would ever flat out tell her that she needed to the touch the fire like the rest of them, but Karma knew that it was only a matter of time before someone had said what they all thought. With London not coming around, Karma and Raven took their direction from Black who gave them one choice, handle Sade or find themselves joining her in a grave.

Sitting inside the semi-crowded Jamaican restaurant Raven and Karma talked casually as they waited for Sade to arrive. Sipping their cocktails as they talked about the latest gossip that was going on in each other's lives now that things had seemed to calm down within the Royal's.

It had been a year since the fall of the old regime, and several months since London decided to take a sabbatical from the family, and with things finally calming down within the Family giving the girls a chance to schedule a luncheon with Sade. Black had made it abundantly clear that they needed to handle the woman before he took matters into his own hands.

Raven had known that if she called and asked her to dinner Sade would agree. If she were working with the Feds, she needed information to report back and being that they hadn't saw each other in a while they needed to see what was up with her.

After agreeing to meet, the duo set out to do what should've been done long ago. After Raven had informed Karma that the day had finally come to tie up the loose ends. Karma knew that it was up to her to take care of the girl that she once called, friend.

"Hey ladies," Sade said as she walked over towards the table. "I'm sorry I'm late. I had an open house that ran longer than expected."

"It's fine," Raven said never looking up from the menu she was holding. "They just brought our drinks. The waitress should be back in a minute."

Sade hung her purse on the back of the chair and took a seat. Placing the napkin that sat atop the place setting on her lap, she smiled as she looked down at her menu. It had been forever since she was able to sit with her girlfriends and enjoy lunch. Everyone was so engulfed in their own endeavors that she hadn't had much time to check in with them to simply catch up.

"So," Sade said looking over the top of the menu. "What's been going on with you girls? I feel like I've missed so much."

Karma and Raven looked Sade over and placed a smile on their faces. Months ago, the duo would've been ready to tell Sade exactly what had been going on in their lives, but those moments had passed.

The weekly lunches and dinners that they had become accustomed to while London was away, still happened, but they had all but counted Sade out. Always giving her an excuse as to why they weren't able to meet up with her, even if it were for a few hours. They'd all been feeding Sade with a long-handled spoon, and even if they were to deny that it wasn't intentional, they all knew that there was something about Sade that they just didn't vibe with anymore.

"Nothing really. Work has been super busy," Karma said placing the menu on the table. Looking around the restaurant aimlessly before bringing her attention back towards the group.

"I understand. I thought you guys were ducking me," Sade said with a chuckle.

"Girl please," Raven said waving her off. "You know how it goes. Everybody has a life and really not enough time to hang out."

"That doesn't stop the three of you from hanging out," Sade retorted. She looked around the table and frowned. "It's like when London came back for some reason you guys don't want to hang with me anymore. I don't know if I did anything wrong or what, but it's fucked up."

Karma started to say something to her statement but the waiter approaching their table caught her words in her throat. Karma smiled as the woman approached the table. The woman was attractive to say the least, with wide hips, and a round ass. Reaching into the apron that was wrapped around her waist removing a note pad and pen, she smiled sweetly.

"Afternoon wah can mi git yuh," she said with a heavy Jamaican accent.

The women ordered their food and watched as the woman disappeared to fulfill their orders. Karma turned her attention towards Sade.

"What's been going on with you?" she asked in a less than pleasant tone.

Sade shrugged as she pushed her side bang from her face. "Same old' same old'," she said. "Just working and running back and forth to New York."

"Really? I didn't know," Karma said looking at her.

"Yes. I've been visiting my parents."

"Really," Raven said looking at Karma.

"Yes, we've been trying to put some things together."

"What things?" Raven asked.

"They've been working on appealing their cases, and I've been trying to find an attorney that would be able to help. I don't think they got a fair deal," she responded.

"What do you mean? I thought they were giving the minimum sentences," Karma asked.

"They were but we're thinking that it could be reduced, and once I find them an attorney, we can come up with some new information then they can definitely receive a lighter sentence."

"What new information?" Raven asked placing the napkin that was on her lap onto the table.

"I don't know yet," Sade said looking at her. "That's why I'm working on it."

Raven looked at Karma and then back towards Sade. "Well, let us know how we can help," she said in a sincere tone.

"So ladies, what's new?" Sade asked.

Karma shrugged, as she began tapping her nails on the table. "Not a lot," Karma answered. "Working on opening a new store in Long Beach."

"That's good. How's London? I thought she was coming?" Sade asked as the waiter appeared with their drinks.

"She's fine. She had meeting that ran later than expected," Raven lied taking a sip from the water in front of her.

"That's good. I've been hearing nothing but good things about her firm," Sade said looking at her. "I haven't saw her in what, two, three months. I wanted to see her. I really miss hanging with all of you."

Raven watched as Karma became uneasy, shifting nervously in her seat. "Other than working and seeing your parents. What's been going on with you?"

"Nothing. Trying to find someone to settle down with," she said taking a sip from the glass in front of her. "I'm ready for kids, a husband. All that shit that we all said we didn't want."

They all laughed and continued to make trivial conversation. The chimes of the door opening caused Karma to look towards the door. She nudged Raven lightly causing her to look at her. Karma motioned with her head towards the door, and Raven's eyes doubled in size. It felt like someone had knocked the wind out of her.

Karma had been staring at the three men as they walked towards the table closest to the door taking a seat. She hadn't noticed that the women at the table eyes had followed her gaze, landing on Face, Vine, and a man she had never saw before in her life.

He was cute, at least from the distance that separated the two. He was a dead ringer for Omari Hardwick the exception of the beard and the swagger that Omari carried in his walk, the man was his doppelganger.

"Is that Face and Vine?" Sade asked turning her head and looking at the girls. The smile that was plastered across her face let them know that she found one of them attractive, but which one was the million-dollar question.

"That's them," Raven said in a matter of fact tone. "Let me find out that these niggas are following y'all."

Karma smirked and shrugged her shoulders. "I didn't know they were coming here. This is just a coincidence."

"Damn he's cute," Sade said turning her head to look back at the men.

"Who?" Raven and Karma said in unison.

"Vine," Sade said in a matter of fact tone. "I wonder if he has a girlfriend."

"Oh shit," Karma said looking at Raven with a smile on her face.

"What? Y'all know something I don't," Sade said.

"Nah," Karma answered. "Vine's available."

"Really?" Raven shrieked.

"Does it really matter?" Karma asked looking at Sade.

"Not really," Sade said looking back towards him. "Whoever he's doing, she must not be much if she let that nigga leave the house with an empty belly and a full nut sack."

Karma chuckled. "Nah his nuts are definitely empty."

"How would you know? You can't tell that just by looking at the man," Sade said looking at her.

"Because when I fucked him this morning, he didn't have shit left to give," she said. She looked at Sade and shook her head before bursting in a fit of laughter.

"So y'all was just gon let me play myself when you know that he's your man," Sade said looking at them.

"Hey," Raven said giggling. "It's not like you ever cared before."

Sade looked at Karma and then Raven, the smile that was on her face seemed fade.

'There's no way she knows,' Sade thought as she looked at her. Karma sat back in her chair as the waitress approached the table and sat their food down in front of them. Karma took in a fork full of the rice and peas and looked at Sade as she placed food into her mouth. The women ate in silence, as Karma kept looking towards Vine who seemed to have his eyes trained on their table.

Placing the napkin on her plate signaling that she was done, she continued to watch the others as they ate.

Sade placed her fork down as she grabbed the glass of water.

"I think I swallowed wrong," she said as she began coughing.

Raven began patting her on the back as Karma watched. It seemed as though the coughing became more intense, and Sade couldn't get it under control. Karma reached into her purse and threw three hundred-dollar bills on the table and stood to her feet.

"Rave," Karma said as she watched her friend continue to pat the others back. "Let's go."

"She's choking to death," Raven said looking at her. Noticing that she was looking at Sade without so much as a care for her wellbeing.

"Oh," she said standing to her feet.

Karma walked over towards where Vine was sitting and looked at him. "I'll see you later," she asked placing her hand on his chin.

"Yeah."

"The wire," she said turning towards the mystery man.

"It's already taken care of," he responded.

"Alright. I'm out," she said as she turned on her heals and walked out of the restaurant. Stepping out into the sunlight, she reached into her bag and removed the glasses she kept inside.

"You could've given me a heads up," Raven said looking at her. "Had me over here thinking the bitch was choking on a damn bone."

"She did," Karma shrugged. "At least that's what it'll look like on the coroner's report. Asphyxiation."

"Wow," Raven said looking at her. "Listen Linda. The next time some shit's about to go down please let me know."

"It made it more believable. I didn't need her last thought to be that her girls turned on her completely. Where to?" Karma asked as they walked through the parking lot.

"Can we go get drunk now. Because this is some shit I need to process," Raven said.

"I need to find some shit to wear for the damn pool party this weekend."

"It's not a pool party," Raven said.

"Bitch it's a pool party," Karma said looking at her.

"It's a housewarming," Raven countered.

"Bitch it's the middle of December and it's eighty-five degrees," Karma snapped placing her hand on her hips. "Does she not have a pool and is it not a party. Put it together we're having a pool party."

"Fine," Raven said walking towards her car. "Let's go to the damn mall. Neiman's is having a sale. But after that you owe me a drink."

"Your treat?" Karma asked looking at her.

Raven looked back towards the restaurant and shook her head. "Yeah it's my treat. Let's go before I change my mind."

## 2017

# <u>*Chapter Twenty*</u>

The gentle sound of his snoring caused her to stir from the slumber that she'd been in. Pulling the goose feathered comforter over her body, she nestled closer into his embrace. For the past five months London and Brandon were inseparable. She'd spent so much time getting to know the man that was hell bent on locking up every member of her family, that she hadn't noticed that she was falling in love with the man.

London had learned his habits, likes and dislikes, leaving nothing left for her to figure out about the man. Only allowing herself to divulge the information she thought he needed to know, never revealing her involvement with the Royals. Brandon seemed to welcome her into his world far easier than she could. The lines were clear from the beginning, but with every passing day they seemed to become blurred.

It wasn't just the physical attraction Brandon was everything that London hadn't dated. He'd taken her on several trips, she'd met his family, and even the gifts that he presented her with were always well thought out and more special than the last. Brandon was smart, funny, handsome, and had made his presence known and felt from the first time he said hello.

When the two first became intimate London actually shed tears, not from the pain his nine inch member that seemed to fill her walls seemingly to the brim almost making her feel as though she wouldn't be able to handle him, but because they had actually made love.

Brandon was a gentle, and attentive lover. He'd created orgasms that were as strong as ocean waves, every time and London couldn't remember the last time she was actually complete with a man.

"Good morning," he whispered pulling her closer to him. He brushed her hair from his face as he kissed the nape of her neck.

"Good morning." London adjusted her head on the pillow and smiled as he pulled her closer to him.

"We have to get ready to head back to the city," he whispered.

"Do we have to? I like it here."

Brandon turned London to face him and kissed her. "I know but we have to get back to the world. The real world."

"But our world is so much better," she said.

Brandon leaned over picking up something off of the nightstand and handing it to her. London looked down at the small black box and smiled.

"You didn't," she said as she sat up in the bed knowing exactly what was in the box.

"I love you London. I know it's soon and sudden, but I want this for the rest of my life. I want you for the rest of my life," he said as he placed his hand over hers.

London opened the box and looked at him. The ten-carat diamond solitaire was flawless, as she watched the diamond sparkle Brandon looked over at her and smiled removing the ring from the box.

"Tell me you'll spend the rest of your life with me," he said grabbing ahold of her left hand. "Will you marry me?"

A single tear fell from her eyes as she shook her head yes. London couldn't deny the fact that she loved Brandon, he was everything she needed in her life. When she was with him, she didn't have to wonder if there was something he was hiding, or if the topic of discussion would be the shit that went on in the streets. No, whenever they were together work was the furthest things from their minds, and they genuinely enjoyed being in each other's presence.

Brandon slid the ring onto her finger and kissed her deeply. London pulled Brandon on top of her and with one hand reached down and grabbed ahold of the nine-inch member massaging him slowly and gently as it became a stiff, hard muscle. Guiding himself towards her entrance he looked at her and smirked, grabbing one of her legs and placing it into the crook of his arm.

"Tell me you love me," he whispered as he ran his dick over her clit causing her to become wet.

London bit down on her bottom lip enjoying the tease but hoping that it would end soon. She needed him to slide in her fast.

"Tell me," he said continuing his game.

"I love you," she said inching her hips off the bed.

Brandon smirked as he entered her forcefully causing her to let out a loud moan. "I love you too," he whispered as he began to dig into her.

Brandon flipped London in every position imaginable, both trading control as they made love well into the afternoon. Once Brandon had let himself go inside of her they both collapsed and the only sounds to be heard were of their breathing, as they fell asleep in each other's arms.

London awoke to the sounds of people scurrying around the room. She felt around in the bed never opening her eyes checking to see if Brandon were still in bed with her, not feeling his body she opened her eyes and looked at the three people that were staring at her.

"Who are you?" she said in a less than pleasant tone.

"Mr. Tyler sent us up here to get you ready for the ceremony," the first woman spoke.

London sat up in the bed and looked at her. She was a white woman with blue hair that was curled only at the ends and were partially covered thanks to the hat she wore. The apron that was wrapped around her waist holding, a comb, brush, and a few hair clips.

London looked at the other two and frowned. One held up a winter white dress, and the other was busy moving around the room setting up a chair that resembled a director's seat, and numerous cases filled to the brim with makeup and all of the supplies.

"What's going on? What ceremony?"

"I thought we'd skip the engagement and go right into the marriage," the baritone boomed from the doorway. London watched as his tall frame stalked over towards the bed. He took a seat atop the plush white comforter and motioned for the crew he'd hired to leave out of the room.

"I didn't know that you were doing any of this," she said looking at him.

"I didn't either," he said with a chuckle. "But I do know that I don't want to spend another day without you being Mrs. Tyler."

London smiled and sat up in the bed. "I love you," she said leaning over and kissing his lips.

"Get up, shower, and let these people do their jobs. I have a few people driving up."

"What people?"

"It's a surprise," he winked as he walked out of the room.

London stood from the bed, stretching her hands over her head. She didn't know what all Brandon had planned, but she was happy as ever. Not knowing whether if marrying this man would play into her plan, as she went about the task of getting ready for the impromptu wedding that he'd planned.

---

Raven sat on the passenger side of Karma's car shaking her head as they pulled up to the house in Napa, California. She couldn't believe the call that she'd received that morning from none other than Brandon Tyler, letting her know that he was going to marry London that day and that he wanted her and any of their close friends at the wedding.

She didn't even bother to ask where he had gotten her number from, as it hadn't come to mind. After hanging up with him, she immediately called Karma and told her that London was getting married later than evening, and that Brandon had invited the two of them to come down.

After the initial shock wore off the two hopped in the car and headed for the address Raven was giving. Pulling in front of the house, the two seemed to gasp simultaneously. The house that Karma had pulled in front of was gorgeous. The house had been completely made out of glass, and resembled the very one from the movie sleeping with the enemy, with exception of the home overlooking the beach the house overlooked three acres of land.

Parking in front of the water feature, Karma and Raven climbed out of the car and headed for the front door. Both women had opted to wear jeans and t-shirts, as to not wrinkle the dresses they'd had on hangers sitting in the backseat of the car.

Neither woman had grabbed their bags as they headed for the house, they first needed to see London, to see if this was part of the plan she'd had. Although, it had been a while since the trio had been in the same room with one another, they couldn't deny the fact that they missed their girl.

The door swung open before Karma could knock on the door, the man who greeted them caught her by surprise. Karma had never laid eyes on him before, and from the look that was plastered across his face when he saw Raven, it couldn't have been no one other than Brandon.

Dressed in a pair of gray slacks, and an off white sweater, his chestnut tone looked as though he were freshly tanned, other than the gold Rolex that was on his wrist he wore no other jewelry, something Karma hadn't seen another man do other than her late uncle Robert.

"You must be Karma," he said extending his hand. "And Ms. Daniels."

Karma shook his hand and nodded yes. "You must be Brandon," she said looking at him.

"Do come in," he said moving to the side so that they could enter the house.

Karma and Raven looked around the space in astonishment as they watched the hired hands transform the living room. Several white pillars sat around the space surrounded by red roses and baby breath flowers, several white chairs with blush ribbon sat in rows surrounding the makeshift alter where the two were to stand during the ceremony. She had to admit that in the short amount of time that Brandon had, he'd gone all out.

"She's upstairs," he said to the women. "I'd escort you up, but she's put me out several times today."

Karma and Raven chuckled nervously. "Well I guess we'll go up and see the bride."

"Sounds good," he said as one of the decorators started in their direction. "If you'll excuse me. She's in the third room on the right."

Raven and Karma watched as the man walked away. Both women climbed the stairs, and headed for the room that Brandon had told them that London was in. Knocking lightly on the door before opening the door, they entered the room both stopped in their tracks.

Standing in a floor length Jason Wu dress that clung to her body like a glove. The dress was covered in lace, and displayed her perfect chocolate complexion, her spiral curls had been straightened and placed into a high bun with crystals decorating the bun, her makeup had been done flawlessly. Five carat diamond studs in ear, and matching diamond necklace around her neck. Both women shed a few tears as they starred at their best friend, who was the perfect image of what a bride should be.

"You have guests," the woman who was helping London with her shoes said.

London turned around and almost fainted when she saw Raven and Karma standing there. She half walked half ran over to her girls wrapping her arms around their necks.

"I didn't know that you guys were coming," she said as tears fell down her cheeks. "I…I'm sorry."

Raven wiped at her face and smiled. "Brandon called this morning and asked us to come."

"So, you guys were the surprise," she said with a giggle.

"Come on," the woman said as she gathered her belongings. "Let's give them the room."

The women watched the people walk out of the room before closing the door. London walked over towards the chair and took a seat. She looked at Raven and Karma with a smile on her face.

"I can't believe that you guys are here," she said as she patted the wet marks on her cheeks.

"I can't believe you're getting married," Karma said looking at her. "London this is all too fast."

"This wasn't part of the plan," Raven said looking at her.

London shook her head and dropped her head. "I know."

"Then what the fuck are you doing?" Karma asked.

London leaned forward in her chair and looked at both women. "It's hard to explain."

"What's so hard to explain? You were only supposed to be with him long enough to divert his attention away from the family," Karma whispered. "This is something totally different."

London sighed. "He's never going to stop coming after the family," she said looking at both of them. "When Black got out, it was like he started working ten times harder to build a case against us."

"So, why the fuck are you still with him?" Karma asked looking at her.

"Because they'll recuse him off the case once they discover what we all know," she said looking at them.

"What's that?" Karma asked confused and pissed.

"That I'm the Queen."

Raven looked at London as a smile crossed her face. Karma looked at both of them and frowned.

"What the fuck is going on, and what the fuck are you smiling about?"

"Not only will he not be able to prosecute the case, but he won't be able to testify against you in open court. That's smart."

London shook her head as she looked at them. "Not only that, but half of the people that work in his office are all now on the Royal's payroll, so we don't have to worry about them working endlessly to destroy us."

"This may just work," Raven said looking at them both. "Ok, but what about Black? Have you spoken to him?"

"No, and I'm glad you mentioned it. I need both of you to take pictures and leak them to LA Confidential. I need Black to hate me if we're going to pull this off."

Karma and Raven looked at one another, and then back towards London.

"Why are you doing this to that man?" Karma asked. "You know he still loves you, despite everything that has happened."

London stood to her feet and headed for the door. "We're almost at the end, and in order for everything to fall the way I need it to. I need Black to want me dead. Any feelings that he may have for me needs to be replaced by hate, if I'm going to save this family," she said turning and looking at them. "Leak the pictures."

They watched as London motioned for the staff to come back into the room and continued about the business of getting herself ready for her wedding. It was supposed to be the happiest day of her life, and also the day that the story of London and Black came to an end.

# _Chapter Twenty-One_

Sitting across from the man London couldn't help but shudder. She'd known him most of her life, and he'd been a friend of her father's. London had gone out of her way to not have any dealings with those her father considered friends being that she didn't know whether or not they were indeed friend or foe.

With all of the craziness that surrounded the family, London no longer had the option of keeping those her father knew at a distance. After the wedding, London had called a meeting, the first meeting with every head of the charters of the Royals, excluding Black.

She didn't let them know the extent of the plan she was working on, but she did offer them a way out. She'd heard through the grapevine that the feds were starting to sniff around due to the number of murders taking place on the East Coast and down South, causing her to question the loyalty of members in those charters.

She'd been given the details surrounding the arrest of Black and the others and been made aware that the State had a witness from within the Royals. He'd given them names, dates, and enough details about the family to have everyone sitting under a jail.

London was surprised when she'd learned that not only had her name never come up on the wiretaps, but the witness didn't mention her or her dealings. That still didn't stop London from hiring a group of killers to find the man, offering them half a million dollars in cash if he never made it to the witness stand.

London knew that all it took was one weak link to tarnish the chain, causing a domino effect. London didn't want to step on Black's toes, but she knew that he hadn't been on top of the family since she'd stepped off with Brandon, and she couldn't blame him. They'd both held a certain responsibility to the family, and both had let the family fall apart because neither knew exactly what it took to lead the organization.

At times she regretted not having her father around, but she knew that he was part of the reason the Royals were filled with disloyal members that made up a Board infiltrated by their enemies. Being that Robert was long gone, London sought out the next best thing.

Salvador Villa had been one of her father's trusted friends, and being that she didn't have her father around to school her on the ins and outs of running a family, she called on him. Under the guise that he was one of her clients, London had spent the better part of two hours telling him everything that had gone wrong in the family. There was nothing that seemed to go in their favor, since the moment London had decided that death was always an option for those that didn't agree with her.

His olive skin tone was wrinkled and shown signs of his age, his short stature put him at eye level with the woman when they stood, his gray hair had been cut short and combed neatly towards the back. Dressed in an Italian made suit that complemented his style, and the cane he used to walk, Salvador Villa, looked every bit of what she envisioned an older Italian man to look like.

Whenever he spoke it caused goosebumps to form over her skin, not because she was afraid of him, but because when he spoke it was with such conviction, not only did he believe the words he spoke, but he needed her to believe them as well.

"I can make all of this go away in the matter of weeks," he said looking at her.

London looked at him, starring into his eyes trying to see if he were going to look away. "What do you mean?"

"You remind me of him," he said.

"Who?"

"Your father. He didn't know what he was doing either and it took him almost five years to do what you've done here today. Five years for him to ask for help."

London sat back in her seat and looked at him. "I'm not naïve enough to know that anything in this life comes free, and I'm not saying yes to anything."

"You will," he said reaching into the pocket of his suit jacket. Removing an envelope and placing it on the table. London picked up the envelope and opened it, removing several papers.

"What's this?"

"I have a few friends that work for the DEA, ATF, and FBI. They're investigating your family, and I'm willing to bet that they'll stop at nothing to have your organization fall," he said looking at her. "I can have all of this wiped away, and you and your family can go back to what you once were."

"And what's that?" she asked confused.

"The Royals are the only organization that has ever come close to competing with the mob, and the only organization that's ran by blacks," he said. "No matter what you may think of them or what you think they're supposed to be. The Royals were meant to be an illegal operation. The legal aspects are just a cover, and you've lost sight of that."

London looked at him and took in every word that he'd said. She'd known that the Royals were on the same tier as the mob, and would surely go down in history as one of the greatest underworld organizations the streets had ever seen, but history could always be rewritten, and as she looked at Salvador she couldn't help but wonder what all he could do to help fix the mess that she'd created.

"If you help me, what do you want in return?" she asked.

He let out a slight chuckle. Reaching into the same pocket that he'd removed the envelope he pulled out a cigar and lighter. Taking a puff from the cigar he looked at her with a slight smile on his face.

"Have you ever been to a shrink?"

# *Chapter Twenty-Two*

Brandon walked into the house feeling the weight of his day. He had been in and out of meetings, with numerous attorneys, officers, and hardened criminals. All he wanted to do at this moment was sit on his couch and enjoy a beer while watching the game.

Once he and London had returned home from the house in Napa Valley, he'd moved out of his downtown loft into the London's townhouse in Manhattan Beach. The transition was effortless, being that London had been welcoming of him moving into the house. Although London's house had enough room for the two of them, Brandon had spoken to her several times about looking for a house. He'd wanted to start a family right away, and being that London wasn't on anyone's birth control he knew that it was only a matter of time before she'd end up pregnant.

Brandon had to admit that the perks of being married were nice. He came home almost every night to a hot meal, the sex was great, and London was almost always eager to help him sort out his day.

Removing the navy jacket of the Kitoni suit that he was wearing and placing it on the railing of the staircase, and his briefcase on the last step, he followed his nose into the kitchen. Brandon watched as London moved around the kitchen, swaying her hips to the Mary J. Blige song that was playing over the stereo speakers.

Walking up behind her, he wrapped his arms around her waist kissing her neck. The Marc Jacobs perfume that she'd put on that morning still present on her neck, as he inhaled her scent.

"How was work?" he asked releasing her.

"It was fine," she said turning around and kissing his lips. "How was your day?"

"It was rough," he said releasing her. Walking over towards the fridge he removed a beer and moved around to the bar stools taking a seat.

"What happened?" she asked genuinely interested in his day.

"I'm trying to build a case against this organization and its starting to seem as though they're untouchable."

London looked at him and smirked. "I'm sure you'll figure something out."

Taking a sip from the beer he shook his head. "I will. What's for dinner?"

"Salmon stuffed with wild rice, broccoli, and salad," she said as she began making their plates.

"Dessert?" he asked eyeing her.

London turned on her heels. Placing the plates on the table, she walked over towards him and wrapped her arms around his neck. "Whatever you want?"

"Can I have it first?" he asked.

Looking over the loose-fitting shorts that London had on, and the oversized t-shirt she wore. Running his hand up her back he knew that she wasn't wearing a bra, and as he placed his hand under her shorts, he used his finger to push her panties to the side and inserted a finger into her.

London closed her eyes knowing what was about to happen, and she wasn't going to stop it even if she wanted to. Sleeping with Brandon had been a bonus that was sure to keep on giving until the moment she decided that she was done with him.

# _Chapter Twenty-Three_

"I'm Dr. Nichols and you are," he said as he extended his hand. London looked at it and then him, and grimaced.

She walked over towards the chair that was opposite his desk and took a seat. Reaching into her oversized bag, she removed her cellphone and looked down at the screen as she began going through her emails.

Thinking back to the initial visit he'd had with the woman he couldn't help but to shake his head. As he listened to the men sitting in the seat that she'd occupied for the past month, tell him that she was the head of a criminal organization he couldn't help but disagree. There was no way that someone that beautiful, someone that well put together, would be capable of the things they claimed that she'd done.

When the men had first approached him it was in connection to a series of drug overdose, by patients. If it hadn't been for the fact that he had begun writing opioid prescriptions to supplement his dwindling practice, he wouldn't be in the predicament that he was now in.

They'd offered him full immunity, and he'd still be able to keep his DEA number so that he would be able to treat the patients who really needed treatment if he helped them gather enough information on the woman who'd come to his office once a week.

He'd tried to tell them that she never said more than the common pleasantries, they didn't believe him. After supplying him with a tape recorder that he was to use during her sessions, the agents let him know that if he couldn't provide them with the information they needed to arrest the woman then he'd be going down for the murders of two of his patients.

Dr. Nichols agreed. He had a wife, child, and a life to think about, and the truth of the matter was he didn't know the woman. So if it were her life for his, he'd always choose himself.

The officers had made it clear that time was limited and he needed to gather the information they'd needed on the woman, and as his receptionist buzzed in letting him know that she was here, he knew that today was the day. Come hell or high water he was going to get the woman to tell him something, anything so that the agents would finally leave his life.

Her Dior perfume entered the room before she did and lingered for hours after her departure. She was extraordinarily beautiful; skin the color of hot chocolate, emerald green doe shaped eyes, full lips with a beauty mark that sat above her upper lip, and auburn colored spiral curls that danced below her shoulders. There wasn't a doubt in his mind that she wasn't aware of how breathtakingly attractive she was, and he knew that from her firm breasts, thick thighs, and hourglass shape that there wasn't a man dead or alive that could deny her of her radiant beauty.

Becoming anxious he cleared his throat and tapped his fingers lightly on the desk. "Can I ask you a question?"

She looked up from her cellphone and stared at him. "What's going on?"

Her voice was soft and almost angelic but carrying a sternness that he noted.

"How long are you going to keep coming here? I mean if you're not actually going to talk during our sessions, I don't see the point."

She placed her cell on the table and crossed her arms across her chest. "I'm only here out of obligation to my husband. It was either this or being committed and of course I chose the latter," she replied.

"So how long do you plan on keeping up this charade?"

---

Black had read every post on the gossip site wondering what the hell was wrong with London. Although the two hadn't spoken in several months, he still loved her, and he knew that deep down she was the one that he wanted to spend his life with. But as he looked at the images of the love of his life smiling and laughing with the enemy, he couldn't help but to feel hatred towards her.

Something from deep within his soul wanted to end London, but he knew that he couldn't. Taking London out would have done nothing to heal his broken heart and bruised ego. True he had fucked up and had a baby outside of their relationship, but London had taken the cake. She'd gone out and married another man. A man that was hell bent on destroying everything that they were.

In his selfish mind London belonged to him, and he was going to do whatever it took to make sure that she ended up right where she belonged, with him.

Sitting in the passenger seat of Vine's black on black Mercedes, he watched as the man walked towards his car. A scowl crossed his face as he thought of the man who was now fucking the woman that belonged to him.

Here it was the man that was trying to take down the Royals, their family, and London had gone out of her way and married him. He didn't believe in coincidences, but he found it mighty strange that London was with the enemy, while the family was taking hits left and right.

London and the girls had been the only people that weren't being faced with jail time and had never seen the inside of a police precinct thanks to the men keeping their names clean.

"What you want me to do?" Vine asked as he looked over at him.

"Follow that nigga and see where he goes," he said looking out of the window. The scowl never leaving his face.

Vine shook his head and pulled into traffic following the red Mercedes. "What's the plan?"

Pulling into an underground parking lot Vine pulled his car into one of the available parking slots. They both sat back in their seats and waited. They watched as he boarded the elevators with two men, and no sooner than he had disappeared she emerged. Both he and Vine watched as she walked by the car. She looked around the garage as she made hurried steps towards her car. Vine looked over at Black who was on the phone and then back towards the woman.

"Long time no hear," he spoke into the phone.

London was silent, other than her breathing Black wouldn't have known that she was on the phone. The sound of her voice caused his heart to ache, he wanted to hop out of Vine's car and grab her, he just wanted to touch her, and if push came to shove, he was going to kill her ass if she gave up the family to be with the nigga she was with.

"We have a problem," she said.

He chuckled lightly, "Well damn. It's nice to hear from you."

"Black, I'm serious. Do you think that you'll be able to meet me?"

London stopped talking and looked at Richard. The look that was on his face was the same one he'd had earlier. She stepped away from the window and headed for his desk, aiming the gun for his head.

Total silence filled the room other than the sounds her heels made as she crossed the floor. Richard looked at her, and then turned away. She was nothing like the woman he thought she was when she'd first come into his office. Instead, she was heartless as the people he'd tried to spend his life getting away from.

Running her hand through her hair, she smirked as she looked at him.

"Where's the recorder?" she asked looking at him.

"I d...don't know what you're talking about," he stammered.

Boom...Boom.

The bullets hit him in the arm twice, and as she kept the gun trained on him, the look of disdain written across her face along with the bullets that penetrated his arm let him know that now was not the time to lie to the woman holding the gun.

"Where's the recorder?" she asked again.

London watched as he reached under his desk, removing a small recording device and throwing it on the table.

"Is this it?" she asked. "This is the only one you have in this office?"

"Y…ye….yes."

London shook her head and grabbed the recorder off the table.

"Yo…you…you don't have to do this," he said noticing that she hadn't lowered the gun.

London titled her head as she looked at him, shaking her head as the faint sounds of water dripping onto the carpet could be heard. "I think I do," she said looking at him.

"But my father," he said.

"Who do you think sent me here?" she said with a chuckle.

"He wouldn't-"

London raised her hand signaling him to be quiet. "You were the reason your father's organization almost fell thirty years ago," she said shaking her head. "And because of that your times up."

Boom...Boom…Boom.

The shots hit him in the chest killing him instantly. London turned on her heels and walked out of the door. Walking towards the elevator she nodded towards the janitor who was still cleaning up the office space.

He looked over at her and placed the empty trash can he was holding back on the floor. Wiping his hands on the blue jumpsuit he began pushing his cart towards her.

"Call me after the cleanup," she said pressing the button calling the elevator.

"I got you," Face said as she stepped into the elevator.

London nodded her head and let out a sigh of relief. After everything that London had done, she now knew that this was only the beginning. Dr. Nichols was the beginning of her to regaining normalcy within the family, and now that she'd taken care of one problem, she still had several others to tend to.

She needed to get the family from out under the feds eye. Now it was time to bring Black up to speed, she didn't know if he would be as receptive to the news and being that she had crossed lines that she shouldn't have crossed, she knew that Black needed to know everything. And there was no better time than now.

Stepping off the elevator London headed towards her car, she looked around the parking garage noticing that the cars that once surrounded her car were gone with the exception of a black Mercedes. The windows were heavily tinted so she couldn't see if anyone was inside the car.

Pressing the button turning off her alarm she climbed inside, leaning over and placing the gun back into the compartment, she noticed him step out of the car making a bee line for her car. The nine-millimeter handgun he was carrying in his hand made her heart drop to her feet.

# *Epilogue*

## *Two Months Later*

LA Confidential here, your one and only source into the scandalous lives of the Royals.

Springtime in the city of Los Angeles, with thousands coming into the city every year with hopes of becoming Hollywood Royalty, residents know that the only royalty worth mentioning are our very own King and Queen.

Being that our Queen who decided that after almost nine months of taking a step down from her reign to venture into a life of a District Attorney's wife has come back into the fold, we're starting to see the rise of one of the greatest duos since the late Stone and Sable.

Although, our King is without his Queen, for the moment, he's been at the top of his game. We're hearing that not only has he been making moves on behalf of his kingdom, but he's doing everything that it takes to bring his Queen back into his house.

All of that's well and good, but let's be real folks, we know why you're here. Yes, it's true we're in the middle of a cold war. With LAPD, the Feds, and the District Attorney all blatantly coming for the Royal's we wonder what our King and Queen will do to protect their family.

Only time will tell if this modern-day tale of Bonnie & Clyde, or should we say, Stone & Sable has what it takes to bring our family through this war. But, until then stay tuned because everything you thought you knew about these two just might turn out to not be true. Soon you'll hate me, L.A. Confidential.

Closing the laptop as a smile spread across her face. She looked around the crowded café, and then towards the two people that sat in the corner staring in her direction. Placing her laptop inside of her bag, she stood to her feet. Grabbing the cup of coffee off the table, she headed for the door.

The gust of wind that had blown through the air caused her spiral curls to blow into her face. Running her perfectly manicured fingers through her hair pushing her curls back, she stepped out into the air.

Her chocolate complexion was without a flaw, almond shaped emerald green eyes that seemed to sparkle under the rays of the sun, stacked in all the right places. The blue Calvin Klein jeans that she wore clung to her hips and thighs as if they were painted on, and the short sleeve v-cut t-shirt that she wore displayed the mounds of her perky 36C cup breasts.

"Aye London," a voice boomed from behind her.

She kept walking as the man kept calling out the name, "London". Feeling someone grab her arm she turned around ready to go off. It was one of the men who had been sitting at the table staring in her direction.

"Damn London," he said looking her over.

"My name's not London," the woman snapped.

"My bad you look just like this girl I know."

She chuckled and extended her hand, "Beauty," she said with a smirk. "Beauty Clark."

He flashed a smile of gold and diamond filled teeth, taking her hand in his. "Everybody calls me Pick."

# This Is The Life Vol. 3:Power Circle Coming Soon